Tales from the
MABINOGION

Tales from the
MABINOGION

Gwyn Thomas and
Kevin Crossley-Holland

Illustrated by Margaret Jones

The Overlook Press
Woodstock, New York

First paperback published in 1996 by
The Overlook Press
Lewis Hollow Road
Woodstock, New York 12498

Library of Congress Cataloging in Publication Data

Thomas, Gwyn, 1936–
    Tales from the Mabinogion.

    Summary: A retelling of the four books of the
Mabinogion, a collection of Welsh medieval tales about
the fears and exploits of legendary Welsh kings and
princes.
    1. Tales — Wales.   [1. Folklore — Wales]
I. Crossley-Holland, Kevin.   II. Jones, Margaret
(Jones of Aberystwyth), ill.   III. Mabinogion.
IV. Title.
PZ8.1.T375Tal   1985   398.2'2'09429   84-14777
ISBN 0-87951-637-2

Printed in Hong Kong

Frontispiece: The Finding of Pryderi (page 26)

THE MABINOGION

The Mabinogion are medieval Welsh tales. The manuscripts in which they are found are about seven hundred years old, but the tales themselves are much older; they had been told – in one form or other – for centuries before they were ever written down. Some of the strange men and women in the stories were, at one time, old Celtic gods. These gods were the gods of the people who lived in Britain before the Romans and the Anglo-Saxons came. The descendants of these people are the Welsh, the Scots, the Irish, the Manx (the people of the Isle of Man), the Cornish, and the Bretons (the people of Brittany, in France). With the coming of Christianity the old gods were gradually forgotten. A dim memory of some of them survives in these stories – in the giant king Bendigeidfran, for example, and in Rhiannon, the mysterious woman on the magic horse. It is in the magicians and in the strange ways of the human characters in these stories that we see shadows of the old gods.

The magic and the wonder of these stories would have held rough warriors and their ladies spellbound in the courts of Welsh kings and princes many centuries ago. Trained story-tellers would have told of the Throne of Arberth and of the enchantment of Dyfed, in the firelit darkness of medieval halls. And some of the stories would have been told by the ordinary people in their simple houses or on a hill on a summer day. In this way some of the old stories became folklore. In the twentieth century we can become our own story-tellers and make the printed words bring back to life Rhiannon and Branwen and Gwydion and their strange world.

These four stories, or four 'branches' or 'parts' as they are called, are the ones which should properly be called 'The Mabinogion'. But this title is usually given to a collection of eleven medieval Welsh tales, those which have survived from what must once have been a great store of tales. In the early Middle Ages a good storyteller would have memorized a large number of such tales and he would certainly have chosen his words carefully to create very vivid impressions in the imaginations of his audience. It may well have been that the storytellers were the highly respected poets of the kings' and princes' courts. It appears that they travelled the country visiting various great houses and monasteries. A visit by a storyteller would have been the cause of great excitement – the sort caused by the visits of the disguised storyteller, Gwydion, in the last of the tales in this book.

Some of the most enthralling characters in the world's greatest stories have their origins in early Welsh poems and tales – King Arthur, for example, and Merlin the magician. That fact will give you some idea of the effectiveness of the kind of storytellers who used to tell such tales as these many centuries ago.

Gwyn Thomas

CONTENTS

PWYLL
being the first branch of the Mabinogion

PWYLL, PRINCE OF DYFED

Pwyll, Prince of Dyfed, was lord of seven regions. While he was at Arberth, one of his chief courts, he thought it would be good to go hunting in the part of his realm called Glyn Cuch. So that evening he set out from Arberth and reached a place called Pen Llwyn Diarwya, and there he remained overnight.

Next day Pwyll got up with the dawn and came to the woods of Glyn Cuch and there he let loose his hounds. He sounded his horn and began the hunt. Pwyll followed his hounds so far into the forest that he lost touch with his friends. And as he listened to the baying of his own pack of hounds, he heard the baying of another pack that sounded different from his own, and this other pack was coming towards his own. Pwyll could see a clearing in the woods, a flat meadow. And as his hounds reached the edge of the meadow he could see a stag running in front of the strange hounds. Near the middle of the meadow these hounds caught the stag and threw it to the ground.

Pwyll looked at the colour of the strange pack of hounds, without even bothering to look at the stag. And of all the hounds he had ever seen, he had seen no hounds the same colour as these. Their coats were shining white and their ears were red. And as their white coats shone, so their red ears gleamed. Pwyll walked up to these strange hounds; he drove them off the stag and began to feed his own hounds on the meat.

While he was busy feeding the hounds, Pwyll saw a knight ride up after the strange hounds on a large, dapple-grey horse. He had a horn hanging from his neck and he wore a hunting cloak of light-coloured material. The knight came up to Pwyll and said to him, 'Lord, I know who you are, but I'm not going to greet you.'

'Is that so!' said Pwyll. 'Perhaps you're so noble you don't have to greet me.'

'You can be sure,' said the knight, 'that it's not my nobility that prevents me from greeting you.'

'Then what prevents you, my lord?' asked Pwyll.

'God knows,' he said, 'it's your impertinence.'

'What impertinence have you seen in me, my lord?' asked Pwyll.

'I never saw a greater lack of courtesy in anyone,' said the knight, 'than that you should drive away the hounds that killed the stag and set your own hounds upon it. Although I'm not going to avenge myself upon you, I'll dishonour you as if you had killed a hundred stags.'

'Now, my lord,' said Pwyll, 'if I've wronged you, I'll buy your friendship.'

'How?' he asked.

'According to your rank, whoever you are.'

'I'm a crowned king in the country I come from.'

'My lord,' said Pwyll, 'good day to you. From what country do you come?'

'From the Other World,' he replied. 'I am Arawn, King of the Other World.'

'My lord,' he said, 'in what way can I win your friendship?'

'This is the way,' said Arawn. 'There's a man whose kingdom lies next to mine, and he is always causing me trouble. His name is King Hafgan. If you will put an end to his enmity – a thing you can easily do – I will be your friend.'

'I'll do that gladly,' said Pwyll. 'And now tell me how I'll do it.'

'Like this,' the King replied. 'I'll be your good friend and arrange for you to take my place in the Other World, and I'll give you the most beautiful woman you've ever seen to live with. I'll make you look exactly like me, so that no servant or officer or anyone who has ever met me will guess that I'm not there. Things will remain like this for a year and a day. Then we'll meet again here.'

'Good,' said Pwyll, 'but if I'm to be in your kingdom for a year, how will I find this man you speak of?'

'I have arranged,' said the King, 'to meet him at the ford one year from tonight. You will be there looking exactly like me. Strike him once only; he cannot live after being struck. And however much he may beg you to strike him a second time, do not agree to it. However many blows I gave him, he'd still be able to fight as well as ever on the following day.'

'Good,' said Pwyll. 'But what shall I do with my own realm?'

'I'll arrange things so that no one in your realm can tell the difference between us,' said Arawn. 'I'll go there in your place.'

'I agree gladly,' said Pwyll, 'and now I'll set out for your kingdom.'

'Nothing will hinder you on your way to my kingdom,' said the King. 'I'll come with you to show you the way.'

Arawn accompanied Pwyll until he could see the court and the houses where Arawn's people lived. 'There you are!' said the King. 'The court and kingdom are yours. Now proceed to the court. Everyone there will know you. And as you see their way of doing things, you'll get used to it.'

Pwyll went on to the court. He could see bedchambers and halls and other rooms, and the most splendid buildings that anyone had ever seen. Then he went to the hall to change his clothes, and squires and young men came to assist him. Each greeted him in turn. And two knights came to take off his hunting garb and dress him in silk clothes of a golden colour.

The hall was made ready. Pwyll looked at the hall guard and the other soldiers as they came into the hall, the fairest and most splendid company that anyone had ever seen, and he saw the Queen with them, the most beautiful woman that anyone had ever set eyes upon. She was wearing a silk dress the colour of bright gold. Inside the hall, everyone went to wash, and then took their places at table.

The Queen sat on one side of Pwyll and an earl (as he imagined) sat on the other. Pwyll and the Queen began to talk. And while he was talking with her he thought he had never met a woman less petty or more gracious. They spent the time eating and drinking and listening to songs. And of all the courts that Pwyll had seen on earth, this had the greatest spread of food and drink, the greatest abundance of gold vessels and priceless gems.

So the time came for them to go to sleep, and off they went – Pwyll and the Queen. As soon as they got into bed, Pwyll turned to face his side of the bed, so that he had his back to the Queen. The next day, they were affectionate and friendly to one another. But however affectionate they were during the day, every night was exactly the same as the first night.

Pwyll spent the year hunting, listening to songs, eating, and talking with his friends, until the night of the combat. And that night everyone in the kingdom of the Other World thought as much about the combat as did Pwyll himself.

Pwyll made his way to the meeting place, accompanied by his noblemen. As soon as he reached the ford across the river a knight stood up and said, 'Now men, listen carefully. This combat is between two kings. Each claims the other's land. All you can do is stand to one side and let them decide it.'

At this the two kings rode to the middle of the ford to meet one another. Pwyll struck Hafgan such a blow on the boss of his shield that it split into two halves and his armour smashed; and Hafgan himself was thrown to the ground a lance- and arm-length behind the rump of his horse. He was mortally wounded. 'Ah! my lord,' said Hafgan, 'what right have you to kill me? I wanted nothing of yours. I know of no cause for you to kill me but, for God's sake, finish what you have begun.'

'My lord,' said Pwyll, 'maybe I'll regret doing what I've done to you. But ask someone else to kill you, I'm not going to do it.'

'Loyal men!' said Hafgan. 'Take me from here. I'm at death's door. I can no longer look after you.'

'And my noblemen!' said Pwyll. 'Take counsel, decide which of these men ought to be my vassals.'

'Lord,' said the noblemen, 'they should all be your vassals, for there is no other king in all the Other World but you.'

'Good,' he said. 'I will receive whoever submits himself to me; and whoever does not will be forced by the sword to do so.'

Hearing this, all Hafgan's men yielded to Pwyll and he took control of the kingdom. By noon on the following day he was recognised everywhere as ruler of the two kingdoms, his own and that of Hafgan.

The Combat of the Kings

That evening, Pwyll rode to Glyn Cuch and his appointed meeting. Arawn, King of the Other World, was already waiting for him. The two were happy to see one another. 'Indeed,' said Arawn, 'may God reward you for your friendship – I have heard about it.'

'Fine,' said Pwyll. 'When you reach your own country, you'll see what I've done for you.'

'May God reward you for everything you've done for me,' said Arawn.

Then Arawn gave back to Pwyll, Prince of Dyfed, his own shape and appearance, and he himself resumed his own shape and appearance. Then Arawn rode towards his court in the Other World, and it gave him great joy to see his people and his guard again for he had not seen them for a year. But they had not missed him, and for them there was nothing new in his return. He passed that day in complete happiness, sitting and talking with his wife and noblemen, until it was time for everyone to go to bed.

Arawn went to bed, and his wife followed him. The first thing he did was to talk to her, and turn to her. She had not been used to this for a year, and she thought, 'What's this? Why is he different tonight from the way he's been for a year?' And she thought for a long time. Arawn woke from a short sleep and spoke to his wife once, twice, three times; but he received no answer. 'Why won't you talk to me?' he asked.

'Well,' she answered, 'I've not talked this much with you in this bed for a year.'

'What!' he said. 'We've talked a lot together.'

'I swear,' she said, 'for a year from last night, from the moment we'd go to bed, I've had no warmth from you, no words, nor your face to me – not to mention anything else.'

Then Arawn thought, 'Indeed, I've had the friendship of a strong and honest man.'

Then he said to his wife, 'My lady, don't get annoyed now, but – as God's my witness – I've not slept with you for a year from last night.' And then he told her the whole story.

'Indeed,' she said, 'you've found yourself a true friend since he's withstood a temptation like that, and been faithful to you.'

'Yes indeed, my lady,' he said. 'I was thinking about that while I was silent.'

'And no wonder!' she said.

Meanwhile Pwyll, Prince of Dyfed, returned to his own realm and country. He soon asked the important people of the country how his government during the last year had compared with previous years. 'Lord,' they said, 'your courtesy was never greater; you were never so kind, never so generous; and things have never been in better order than they've been this year.'

'As God's my witness,' he said, 'you should thank the man who has been here with you. This is what happened . . .' And then Pwyll told them the whole story.

'Fine, lord,' they said. 'Thank God you enjoyed that kind of friendship. And the kind of government we've had this year – you won't take it away from us?'

'I won't, by God,' said Pwyll.

From then on Pwyll and Arawn began to strengthen their friendship, with one sending to the other horses and hounds and hawks and whatever precious thing he thought would please the other. And because Pwyll went to the Other World that year, and ruled there so successfully, and made two kingdoms one through his bravery, he came to be called, 'Pwyll, King of the Other World'.

Once upon a time Pwyll was in Arberth, one of his chief courts. A feast had been prepared and many people were with him there. After the first sitting had eaten, Pwyll got up to stretch his legs, and he walked towards the top of a hill above the court called the Throne of Arberth. 'My lord,' said one of his courtiers, 'the remarkable thing about the Throne is this: if a nobleman once sits on it, he'll not be able to leave without one of two things happening – either he'll be injured and hurt, or he'll see a wonder.'

'I'm not afraid of being injured and hurt amongst as many people as this,' said Pwyll. 'But it would please me greatly to see a wonder. I'll go and sit on the Throne.'

So Pwyll went to sit on it. And as everyone was sitting there they saw a woman riding a grey-white horse many hands high, a woman wearing silk the colour of bright gold. She was coming along the road that passed by the Throne. The horse seemed to move quite slowly, without varying its speed, until it was almost opposite the Throne. 'Ah!' said Pwyll. 'Do any of you recognise the horsewoman?'

'No, my lord,' they said.

'I want someone to go to meet her and find out who she is,' he said.

So a man got up and stepped forward. But as he came to meet her, she went past him. He pursued her as quickly as any man could on foot. But the greater his haste, the further she was from him. And when the man realised it was not worth his chasing after her, he returned to Pwyll and said to him, 'My lord, it's no use anyone on foot pursuing her.'

'Is that so!' said Pwyll. 'Go to the court then, and take the fastest horse you know of, and gallop after her.'

The man took the fastest horse, and off he went. He reached a level plain and spurred on his horse. But the harder he spurred the horse, the further she was from him. Yet the woman still moved at the same unvarying speed she had moved at before. His horse began to slow down. And when he realised his

A Woman Dressed in Gold

horse was tired of galloping, he returned to the place where Pwyll was. 'My lord,' he said, 'it's no use anyone going after that lady. I don't know of a faster horse in the kingdom than this one but, even so, it was not worth my pursuing her.'

'Is that how it is?' said Pwyll. 'There's something magic here. We'll go back to the court.'

And back to the court they went and so the day passed. The next day, they got up and spent the day in the usual way until it was time to go to eat. After the first sitting Pwyll said, 'Now then, those who were there yesterday can come to the top of the Throne again. And you,' he said to one of his young men, 'bring with you the fastest horse you know from the field.' So the young man did that. Off they went to the Throne, and the horse went with them.

While they were sitting there they saw the woman on the same horse, wearing the same dress, coming along the same road. 'Here's the same horsewoman as yesterday,' said Pwyll. 'Be ready, lad, to find out who she is.'

'My lord,' he said, 'I'll do that gladly.'

At that the horsewoman came up opposite them. The young man mounted the horse; but before he had settled himself properly into the saddle she had gone past so that there was some distance between them. But she was moving no more quickly than the previous day. So the young man let his horse amble, and was quite confident he would catch the horsewoman. He was wrong about that. So then he let his horse have its head and quickened into a gallop, but he drew no closer to her than if his horse were walking. The more he whipped his horse, the further she was from him. When the young man realised that it was no use his pursuing her, he came back to the place where Pwyll was. 'My lord,' he said, 'you saw that this horse galloped as fast as he could.'

'I saw it was no use your pursuing her,' said Pwyll. 'But, as God's my witness, that horsewoman must have some business with someone here if only she were not so obstinate. We'll go to the court.'

So they returned to the court and spent that evening singing and feasting until everyone was well contented. And the next day they whiled away the hours until it was time to go to eat. And after eating, Pwyll said, 'Where are those people who went to the top of the Throne yesterday?'

'Here we are,' they said.

'We'll go to the Throne again,' he said. 'And you,' he said to his ostler, 'saddle my horse carefully, and bring it to the road, and bring my spurs with you.' And the ostler did that.

So they climbed and sat on the Throne. They were not there long before they saw the horsewoman coming along the same road as before, looking the same and moving in the same way. 'Now, lad!' said Pwyll, 'I can see the horsewoman. Bring me my horse.' No sooner had Pwyll mounted than the woman rode past him. Pwyll turned after her, and gave his prancing horse its head. He thought he would catch her on the second or third bound. But he was no nearer to her than before. He forced his horse to go as fast as it could, but he realised it was useless to pursue her.

Then Pwyll called, 'Lady! For the sake of the man you love most, wait for me.'

'I'll wait gladly,' she said, 'and it would have been far better for the horse if you'd asked this to start with.' The girl drew in her reins and lifted her veil and looked at Pwyll and began to talk with him. 'My lady,' said Pwyll, 'where do you come from and what is the purpose of your journey?'

'To go about my business,' she said. 'And I'm glad to see you.'

'Welcome to you,' he said.

And then Pwyll thought that the face of every girl and woman he had ever seen was ugly compared to her face. 'My lady,' he said, 'will you tell me about your business?'

'Yes, of course,' she said. 'My most important business is to see you.'

'As far as I'm concerned,' said Pwyll, 'that's the best business you could have. And will you tell me who you are?'

'Yes, my lord,' she said. 'I am Rhiannon, daughter of Hefeydd the Old, and I'm to be given to a man against my will. I have not accepted any husband until now because I'm in love with you. And I will not accept any other husband unless you reject me. I've come here to discover your answer.'

'As God's my witness,' said Pwyll, 'here's my answer: if I had my choice of all the women and girls in the world, you would be my choice.'

'Fine,' she said, 'if that's what you will, arrange to meet me before I'm given to another man.'

'The sooner, the better for me,' said Pwyll. 'Arrange the meeting where you will.'

'I'll do that, my lord,' she said. 'A year from this night, I'll arrange for a feast to be prepared for you in the court of Hefeydd the Old.'

'Splendid,' he said. 'I'll be there.'

'My lord,' she said, 'take care of yourself and remember to keep your word. I'm going now.'

Then they parted, and Pwyll returned to his soldiers and followers. And however much they asked about the girl, he would tell them nothing and would change the subject.

The year passed; it was time to go to meet Rhiannon. Pwyll prepared himself, one of a hundred horsemen, and away he went towards the court of Hefeydd the Old. When he came to the court he was welcomed warmly. Many people had gathered there; there was rejoicing, the feast was ready, and liberal gifts were given as he directed. Then the hall was prepared and the company went to the tables. Hefeydd the Old sat on one side of Pwyll and Rhiannon on the other, and everyone else sat according to his rank. They ate and talked and enjoyed themselves.

And at the beginning of the merrymaking after the feast a tall and regal young man walked into the hall. His hair was auburn and he was dressed in silk. When he reached the dais he greeted Pwyll and his friends.

'A royal welcome to you, friend,' said Pwyll. 'Seat yourself.'

'I won't sit,' said the man. 'I've a request to make, and I must attend to it.'

'Do that, and welcome,' said Pwyll.

'My lord,' he said, 'I have come to make a request of you.'

'Whatever you ask, I'll give it to you if I can.'

'Oh!' said Rhiannon. 'Why did you answer like that?'

'Those were his words, my lady,' said the man, 'and he has spoken them before noblemen.'

'Friend,' said Pwyll, 'what do you want?'

'Tonight you're going to sleep with the woman I love more than anyone. I've come to ask for her, and for this wedding feast here.'

Pwyll fell silent. There was nothing he could say.

'Be quiet as long as you will,' said Rhiannon, 'no man was ever such a fool as you.'

'My lady,' he said, 'I didn't know who he was.'

'This is the man to whom I was to be given against my will,' she said. 'He is Gwawl, son of Clud, a wealthy man who has many soldiers. Since you've spoken as you did, give me to him – otherwise people will make fun of you.'

'My lady,' he said, 'what kind of answer is that? I'll never do that.'

'Give me to him,' she said, 'and I'll ensure he never has me.'

'How?' asked Pwyll.

'I'll give you a small bag,' she said. 'Keep it safely. When he asks for the feast and all the wedding preparations, tell him they're not yours to give. Say that I have given this feast to the soldiers and the company. As for me,' she said, 'I'll make an agreement with him to marry him exactly one year from tonight. Now at the end of the year, have this bag with you – and wait with your knights in the orchard up there. While he's in the middle of his merrymaking, come in by yourself in ragged clothes, with this bag in your hand. Ask for nothing except that the bag be filled with food. I'll arrange things so that the bag will be no fuller even if all the food and drink in these seven regions is put into it. After a lot of food and drink has been thrown into the bag, he will ask, "Will your bag ever be full?" You will say, "No, not unless a very rich and important man will get up and tread down the food in the bag and say 'Enough has been put in here'." Then,' said the woman, 'I'll get Gwawl to go and tread on the food in the bag. When he comes, turn the bag so that he is head over heels inside it. And then knot the laces. You'll need to have a loud horn hanging round your neck; when he has been tied inside the bag, sound your horn as a sign to your knights. When they hear the horn they must attack the court.'

'My lord,' said Gwawl, 'it's high time I had your answer about what I've asked for.'

'Whatever is mine you can have entirely,' said Pwyll.

'Friend,' said Rhiannon for her part, 'I've given this feast and the wedding preparations to the men of Dyfed and the retinue of soldiers and the company here. I'll not allow them to be given to anyone else. But, a year from tonight, a feast will have been prepared here for you, friend, so that you can marry me.'

And Gwawl went to his own country, and Pwyll went to Dyfed.

The year passed until it was time for the feast in the court of Hefeydd the Old. Then Gwawl, son of Clud, came to the feast that had been prepared for him. He went to the court and was welcomed there. Pwyll, King of the Other World, also came – he went to the orchard with one hundred knights, exactly as Rhiannon had instructed, and he had the bag with him. Pwyll put on ragged clothes and old shabby shoes. When he heard the merrymaking after the eating he walked into the hall. When he reached the dais he greeted Gwawl and his company of men and women.

'God's blessing on you, and welcome,' said Gwawl.

'My lord,' he said, 'may God repay you. I'm a man who has some business to do with you.'

'Welcome to your business,' said Gwawl. 'And if you ask for anything reasonable, you're most welcome to it.'

'My request is quite reasonable, my lord,' he said. 'I ask only out of need. What I'd like to have is this bag full of food.'

'You're not asking for much,' said Gwawl, 'and you can have that gladly. Bring him food.'

And a large number of servants got up and began to fill the bag. But in spite of all that was thrown into it, the bag was no fuller than before.

'Friend,' said Gwawl, 'will your bag ever be full?'

'No, as God's my witness,' said he, 'never, in spite of all that's thrown into it, unless a nobleman who owns lands and riches will get up and tread the food in the bag with his two feet saying, "Enough has been put in here".'

'And you, my fine man,' said Rhiannon to Gwawl, 'get up this instant.'

'Gladly,' said Gwawl.

He got up and put his two feet in the bag. Then Pwyll turned the bag so that Gwawl was head over heels inside it, he drew up the laces and knotted them, and then he sounded his horn. And at that his company of soldiers attacked the court and held all those men who had come with Gwawl and put them in chains. And Pwyll cast off his rags and shabby shoes.

As each of the soldiers came into the hall, he gave the bag a kick or a beating

The Beggar at the Feast

with a stick, and asked, 'What's in here?'

'A badger,' the others said. And as each soldier reached the hall, he asked, 'What's this game you're playing?'

'The game of badger-in-the-bag,' they would reply.

And it was here that the game of badger-in-the-bag was first played.

'My lord,' said the man inside the bag, 'if you'd listen to me – killing me in a bag is not a worthy death for me.'

'My lord,' said Hefeydd the Old, 'he's telling the truth and it's right that you listen to him; that is not a fitting death for him.'

'All right,' said Pwyll, 'I'll follow your advice as to what I should do with him.'

And then Rhiannon said, 'I'll give you some advice: you're now in a position where it's your duty to satisfy the people and musicians who ask you and beg you for things. Let him take your place in the giving of gifts, and make him swear that he will never reclaim these gifts from you, nor avenge himself on you; that will be sufficient punishment for him.'

'He can have all that,' said the man inside the bag.

'I'll agree to that gladly,' said Pwyll, 'if that's the advice of Hefeydd and Rhiannon.'

'That is our advice,' they said.

'And I agree to it,' said Pwyll. 'Now! Who will stand witness for Gwawl?'

'We'll stand witness until his own men are free,' said Hefeydd.

Then Gwawl was set free from the bag and his chief men were unchained. 'Now ask Gwawl for his witnesses,' said Hefeydd. 'We know the men he ought to choose.'

And Hefeydd counted the witnesses.

'State your terms,' said Gwawl.

'What Rhiannon has just said is good enough for me,' said Pwyll.

So the witnesses agreed on those terms.

'Indeed, my lord,' said Gwawl, 'I am hurt; I've sustained great wounds and I must bathe them and have them dressed. I'll go, with your permission. And I'll leave noblemen here to respond on my behalf to all the people who petition you.'

'Fine,' said Pwyll. 'Do that.'

And then Gwawl went towards his kingdom.

The hall was prepared for Pwyll and his company, and the company of the court of Hefeydd the Old. And they all took their places at the tables. Each one sat in the same place that he was sitting in a year before. And Pwyll and Rhiannon went to their room and spent that night pleasantly.

'My lord,' said Rhiannon at dawn, 'get up and distribute gifts to the musicians and, today, don't refuse anyone who asks for a gift.'

'I'll do that gladly,' said Pwyll, 'today, and for as long as this feast lasts.'

Pwyll got up and told his servants to call for silence so that he could invite the musicians and anyone who wanted anything to come forward. He told the company that they could all have whatever they desired. And he was as good as his word.

No one was refused anything for as long as the feast lasted. And when the feast came to an end, Pwyll said to Hefeydd, 'My lord, with your permission, I'll start for Dyfed tomorrow.'

'Fine,' said Hefeydd. 'God speed you, and arrange for a time for Rhiannon to follow you.'

'As God's my witness,' said Pwyll, 'we'll go from here together.'

'Is that what you want, my lord?' asked Hefeydd.

'Indeed it is,' said Pwyll.

The following day they travelled towards Dyfed and went to the court of Arberth where a feast had been prepared for them. A gathering of the important men and women of the country met them there. Rhiannon allowed no one to leave without giving him a beautiful gift, either a brooch, or a ring, or a precious gem.

And they ruled the country happily that year and the next year. But during the third year people began to look unhappy and sad because they saw the lord they so loved, their own king and foster-brother, had no heir. They asked Pwyll to talk with them and met him at Preselau in Dyfed. 'My lord,' they said to Pwyll, 'you're not as young as some of us, and we fear your wife cannot give you an heir. Take another wife so that you may have an heir. You will not,' they said to him, 'last forever. And though you may be content without an heir, we're not ready to tolerate that.'

'True enough,' said Pwyll, 'we won't be together long, and accidents may happen. But leave the matter with me until the end of a year; we'll meet together one year from now, and then I'll follow your advice.'

This arrangement was accepted.

Before the time of the meeting a son was born to Pwyll at Arberth. On the night he was born women were brought in to look after the baby and his mother. But these women fell asleep, and so did Rhiannon, the son's mother.

It happened like this. There were six women there, and they kept watch for the first part of the night but before midnight every one of them fell asleep. Towards daybreak they awoke. They looked in the cradle where they had placed the baby, but there was no sign of it. 'Oh!' said one of the women. 'The baby's gone!'

'What are we to do about it?' said another.

'What?' said the rest of them.

And one said, 'There's a hound bitch with her puppies here. We'll kill some of the puppies and rub Rhiannon's face and hands with the blood; then we'll throw their bones in front of her and swear it was she herself killed the baby.

She won't be able to argue against the six of us.' They all agreed to this plan.

When it was getting light Rhiannon woke and said, 'Ah, women, where's the little one?'

'My lady,' they said, 'don't ask us for the little one. We're black and blue all over after struggling with you; and in truth we've never seen such fighting spirit in any woman. But it was no good. You yourself have destroyed your son, and don't ask us about him.'

'Poor women,' said Rhiannon, 'for the sake of God, who knows all things, don't accuse me falsely. God, who knows all things, knows that you're wronging me. If you're afraid, I swear that I'll defend you.'

'Indeed,' they said, 'we're not going to be wronged to shield someone else.'

'Poor women,' Rhiannon said, 'no wrong will come from telling the truth.' But whatever she said, with words fair and pitiful, the women only gave her the same reply.

Now Pwyll got up, and so did his soldiers and the company, and the disaster could not be hidden from them. The story spread through the country and all the noblemen heard it. And the noblemen met, and sent messages to Pwyll asking him to send away his wife as a punishment for the murder of her baby.

'They have only one reason for asking me to send away my wife,' said Pwyll, 'and that is if she has no children. But I know that she has a child, and I'll not send her away. And if she has done wrong, then she will have to accept the proper punishment for it.'

Rhiannon summoned learned men and wise men to her side. Then she decided she would rather accept her punishment than argue with the women. And the punishment imposed on her was that she was to stay in that court of Arberth for seven years. There was a mounting-block outside the gates of the court and she had to sit there every day and tell her story to every passer-by if she thought they did not already know it. Then she had to offer to carry visitors and pilgrims on her back (any who were willing) into the court. But it was a rare thing for anyone to allow himself to be carried. And this is how she spent part of this time.

At this time the lord of Gwent Is Coed was Teyrnon, and he was the best man in the world. In his court there was a mare. And there was nothing in the kingdom – neither horse nor mare – that was more beautiful than she. Every year, on the eve of May Day, she would give birth to a foal, but no one knew what became of it. Teyrnon had a talk with his wife one evening. 'Listen,' he said, 'we're feeble things to allow our mare's foals to disappear every year, and to let them all be taken.'

'What can we do about it?' she asked.

'It's the eve of May Day,' he said, 'may God punish me if I don't find out

As Rhiannon Lay Sleeping

what evil it is that spirits the foals away.'

Teyrnon had the mare brought indoors. He armed himself and began to keep watch. Towards the beginning of the night the mare gave birth to a large, sturdy foal that immediately stood up on its four legs. Teyrnon got up to examine the foal and, while he was looking at it, he heard a great noise; and after the noise a great claw came through the window of the building and seized the foal by its mane. Teyrnon took his sword and struck off the arm between wrist and elbow so that the part of the arm with the foal in its grasp fell inside the building. And then Teyrnon heard a great noise and a shriek together. He opened the door and ran after the noise. He could not see what was causing the noise because the night was so dark; but he rushed after it and chased it. Then he remembered that he had left the door open, and went back. And lying by the door there was a little baby wrapped up in silk. He picked up the little baby boy and saw that he was strong for his age.

Teyrnon bolted the door and went to the room where his wife was. 'My lady,' he said, 'are you sleeping?'

'No,' she replied. 'I was asleep but I awoke when you came in.'

'Here's a baby,' he said, 'if you want him: something you've never had.'

'My lord,' she said, 'where does he come from?'

'I'll tell you everything,' said Teyrnon and he told her the whole story.

'My lord,' she said, 'what sort of clothes is the baby wearing?'

'Silk clothes,' said Teyrnon.

'He's the child of noble people,' she said. 'My lord, I'd be glad to have women speak up and say I gave birth to a child, if that is what you wish.'

'I'll agree readily with you about that,' he said. And that is what they did. They had the child baptised and called him Gwri Golden Hair since what hair there was on his head was as yellow as gold.

The child was brought up in the court until he was two years old. Before he was one he was walking well and was bigger than a child of three – that is, a child of three who is big for his age! At the end of the second year he was as big as a boy of six. And before the end of the fourth year he used to implore the grooms to allow him to take the horses to water.

'My lord,' said his wife to Teyrnon, 'where is the foal you saved that night you found the baby?'

'I gave him to the grooms and told them to look after him,' he said.

'My lord, wouldn't it be a good thing for you to have it trained and given to the boy?' she said. 'It was on the very night you found the boy that the foal was born and you saved it.'

'I've nothing against that,' said Teyrnon. 'I'll allow you to give it to him.'

'My lord,' she said, 'may God reward you. I'll give it to him.'

And the horse was given to the boy. Teyrnon's wife told the trainers and grooms to take care of the horse and have it trained by the time the boy was old enough to ride, and to bring her regular reports about how the horse was coming on.

During this time Teyrnon and his wife heard the news about Rhiannon and her punishment. And because he had found a baby, Teyrnon made a point of keeping his ears open and closely questioning travellers. From many of those who came to the court he heard great complaints about Rhiannon's pitiful punishment. Teyrnon thought about this and looked closely at the child. It struck him that he had never seen a son and father look so alike as the child and Pwyll, King of the Other World. He knew well what Pwyll looked like for he had paid homage to him for a number of years. As a result of this Teyrnon began to worry about how unfair it was for him to keep the boy with him when he knew he was another man's child. On the first occasion he was alone with his wife, he told her that it was not right for them to keep the boy with them and, as a result, cause so much pain to so good a lady as Rhiannon, especially as the boy was the child of Pwyll, King of the Other World.

Teyrnon's wife agreed to send the boy to Pwyll. 'And we can win three things through doing this,' she said. 'Gratitude and reward for releasing Rhiannon from her punishment; gratitude from Pwyll for bringing up the boy and taking him back to him; and the third thing is this – if the boy grows to be a man of honour, he will be our foster-child, and will do the best he can for us.' So they agreed on this.

The very next day Teyrnon prepared to leave with two knights, taking the boy with them as a fourth – on the horse that Teyrnon had given to him. They travelled towards Arberth and it did not take them long to get there. When they approached the court they could see Rhiannon sitting by the mounting-block. When they drew close to her she called out, 'Ah, my lords, go no further. I'll carry each one of you to the court. That's my punishment for killing my own child.'

'Lady,' said Teyrnon, 'I don't think that anyone here will allow you to carry them.'

'Let who will be carried,' said the boy, 'I shan't.'

'Indeed,' said Teyrnon, 'we won't either.'

And they came to the court and were warmly welcomed. Pwyll had just returned from travelling around Dyfed, and was glad to see Teyrnon. Then they went to the hall to wash, and took their places at the table. Teyrnon sat between Pwyll and Rhiannon, and Teyrnon's two friends sat above Pwyll with the boy between them. Then Teyrnon told his whole story about his mare and the boy, and how they – Teyrnon and his wife – adopted the boy as their own child and brought him up.

'And there is your son, lady,' said Teyrnon. 'And whoever has told a lie about you has done great wrong. When I heard about your punishment, I was sad and began to worry. And I don't think there is a single person in all this company who will not recognise that this boy is Pwyll's boy.'

'There's no one here who doubts it at all,' said everyone.

'As God's my witness,' said Rhiannon, 'if that were true, my care would be at an end.'

'My lady,' said Pendaran Dyfed, 'you've chosen a good name for your boy – Pryderi, meaning "my care". The name that suits him best is Pryderi, son of Pwyll, King of the Other World.'

'It may be that his own name suits him better,' said Rhiannon.

'What name?' asked Pendaran Dyfed.

'Gwri Golden Hair is the name we gave him,' said Teyrnon.

'Pryderi,' said Pendaran Dyfed, 'shall be his name.'

'That is best,' said Pwyll, 'to take the boy's name from the words his mother spoke when she had good news about him.' And they agreed on that.

'Teyrnon,' said Pwyll, 'God reward you for bringing up this boy. And if he grows to be a man of honour, it is right he should repay you.'

'My lord,' said Teyrnon, 'no one in the world will be more sad to lose him than the woman who brought him up. It's right he should remember what I and this woman did for him.'

'As God's my witness,' said Pwyll, 'I'll defend your kingdom for as long as I'm able to defend my own. And if Pryderi himself becomes the king here, it'll be even more fitting for him to protect you than it is for me. Now if you and all these noblemen here agree, we'll give the child into the care of Pendaran Dyfed. And you'll be his friends and foster-parents.'

'That is a fine proposal,' said everyone.

So the boy was given to Pendaran Dyfed and the noblemen of the country came to keep him company. Then Teyrnon left with his friends for his own country with love and joy. He did not go without being offered the most beautiful gems and the best horses and dogs. But he accepted nothing.

Then they all lived in their kingdoms, and Pryderi, son of Pwyll, King of the Other World, was brought up with care as he deserved, until he was the most handsome and comely and skilled young man in the kingdom. They lived in that way for one year after another until the life of Pwyll, King of the Other World, came to an end and he died. Then Pryderi ruled successfully over the seven regions of Dyfed, loved in his kingdom and by everyone about him. And in due course he conquered the three regions of Ystrad Tywi and the four regions of Ceredigion: and these are called the seven regions of Seisyllwch. And Pryderi, son of Pwyll, King of the Other World, busied himself with these conquests until he thought about taking a wife. And the woman he chose was Cigfa, daughter of Gwyn the Resplendent, from the very best family of this island.

And that is how this branch of the Mabinogi ends.

BRANWEN
being the second branch of
the Mabinogion

BRANWEN, DAUGHTER OF LLŶR

Bendigeidfran, son of Llŷr, was chosen King of the Island of Britain, which was called 'the Island of the Mighty'; and he was crowned in London. One afternoon he was in Harlech, one of his courts, and he was sitting on the Rock of Harlech, looking out over the sea. His brother Manawydan was with him, as were his two half-brothers, Nisien and Efnisien, and other noblemen besides – a whole company, as befits a king.

These two brothers were the sons of a man called Euroswydd, and their mother was Bendigeidfran's mother, Penarddun. One of them was a good young man; he would make peace between warring armies. This was Nisien. But the other caused emnity even between the two brothers Bendigeidfran and Manawydan, and that at a time when they were most friendly. His name was Efnisien.

While they were sitting on the Rock, they could see thirteen ships coming from the south of Ireland and making towards them. The ships were moving steadily and swiftly, with the wind behind them, and quickly approaching the shore. 'I can see ships over there,' said the King, 'and they're running towards the shore. Order the men to arm themselves and go to see what they want.'

The men armed themselves and went down towards the shore. After seeing the ships close at hand they were all sure that they had never seen ships that were more resplendent – each flew brave and beautiful pennants of silk.

And then one of the ships drew ahead of the others and they could see a shield being raised above the bulwarks, and the tip of the shield was held upwards – a sign of peace. Then the armed men drew nearer to them so that they could talk to each other. The men on board the ship put out boats and rowed towards the shore and greeted the King. And, sitting on the Rock high above them, the King could hear every word they said.

'God bless you,' said the King, 'and welcome. Whose ships are these? And who is leader among you?'

'My lord,' they said, 'it is Matholwch, King of Ireland, who is here; these are his ships.'

'What does he want?' asked the King. 'Does he mean to come ashore?'

'He has a request to make of you, my lord,' they said, 'and he won't come ashore if his request is not granted.'

'What is his request?' asked the King.

'He wants to unite your family and his,' they replied. 'He has come to ask for Branwen, daughter of Llŷr, as a wife for himself and, if you agree to this, he wants to unite the Island of the Mighty and Ireland so that they will both be stronger.'

'Good,' said Bendigeidfran. 'Let him come ashore, and we will discuss the matter amongst ourselves.'

The reply was taken to Matholwch. 'I'll go gladly,' he said.

Matholwch came ashore and was made welcome. What with his troop of men and Bendigeidfran's company, a large crowd of people gathered in the court at Harlech that night.

On the very next day a council was held. And the decision taken was that Branwen should be given as a wife to Matholwch. They agreed to meet in Aberffraw for her wedding, and they all set out from Harlech. The two companies made for Aberffraw in this way – Matholwch and his men in their ships, Bendigeidfran and his men overland.

When they arrived in Aberffraw, they soon sat to the feast and everyone took his proper place. And this is how they sat: Bendigeidfran, King of the Island of the Mighty; then Manawydan, son of Llŷr, on one side of him and Matholwch on the other, with Branwen by his side. And they were not in a house, but in great tents; there was not enough room in any house for Bendigeidfran.

The feast began. And after eating, they started to talk. And when everyone realised they would do better to sleep than to continue feasting, they all went off to sleep. And that night Matholwch slept with Branwen.

The following day, all the company of the court got up, and the steward and his officers began to talk of places where they could billet the horses and servants. And they were put in various places all over the country.

One day Efnisien – the quarrelsome brother already mentioned – came to the stable housing Matholwch's horses, and he asked whose horses they were.

'These are the horses of Matholwch, King of Ireland,' was the reply.

'What are they doing here?' he asked.

'They're here because Matholwch, King of Ireland, is here – and he has married your sister. And these are his horses.'

'So that's what they've done with such a fine girl, and she my sister,' said Efnisien. 'Well, they couldn't have insulted me more. They've given her away without my consent.'

Then Efnisien made for the horses and cut off their lips to the teeth, and their ears flush with their heads, and their tails down to their cruppers; and where he could get hold of their eyelids he cut them to the bone. He maimed the horses in this way so that not one of them was of any use.

Now Matholwch came to hear how his horses had been maimed and made useless.

'Indeed, my lord,' said one of his servants, 'they have disgraced you and

The Marriage of Branwen

that's exactly what they meant to do.'

'God knows,' said Matholwch, 'it seems strange to me that they mean to disgrace me after giving me such a fine girl as Branwen for a wife; such a noble woman, and one so dear to everyone.'

'My lord,' said another one, 'later you can find out for yourself whether they meant to disgrace you, but now you've no choice but to make for your ships.'

So then Matholwch made his way to his ships.

Now Bendigeidfran heard that Matholwch was leaving the court, without asking permission to do so. He sent messengers to him to ask the reason. These men caught up with Matholwch and asked him what he intended to do, and why he was leaving.

'As God is my witness,' Matholwch said, 'I would never have come here if I had known what was going to happen. I have been deeply insulted. No one ever made a worse journey than this. What has happened to me here is beyond understanding!'

'Why is that?' they asked.

'First Branwen, the sister of the King of the Island of the Mighty, is given to me, and then I'm insulted. What is so strange is that this damage wasn't done *before* such a fine girl was given to me.'

'God knows, my lord,' they said, 'it was not our king's wish, nor the wish of any man in his council, that you should be disgraced in this way. And even though this is a great insult to you, it is even more of a disgrace to Bendigeidfran.'

'I agree with that,' said Matholwch, 'but, even so, that does not undo my disgrace.'

The messengers returned with this reply to Bendigeidfran and repeated Matholwch's words.

'Indeed,' said the King, 'it will do us no good if he leaves here feeling hostile. We won't allow him to go in this way!'

'No, my lord,' they said, 'send messengers after him again.'

'I will,' he said. 'Manawydan, son of Llŷr, and Hefeydd the Tall, and Unig Valiant Shield, get up and gallop after him! Tell him he shall have a sound horse for every one that was maimed. And above that, to compensate him for the insult to his honour, he shall have a silver staff as thick as his little finger and as tall as himself, and a gold plate as wide as his face. And tell Matholwch what sort of man it is who did this to disgrace him, and tell him it was against my will; tell him that the man who did this is my half-brother and that, because of this, it isn't easy for me to kill him or punish him. Ask Matholwch to meet me. Tell him I'll make peace with him in any way he wishes.'

Away went the messengers after Matholwch, and they gave him this message in a spirit of friendship, and he listened to them.

'Men,' he said, 'let us take counsel.'

They talked amongst themselves and this is what they decided: if they refused the offer, they might very well end up not with more compensation but with more disgrace. So Matholwch decided to accept the offer, and he and his company returned peacefully to the court. Tents were pitched for them in accordance with the proper plan of a hall, and they went to eat. They all took their places there as they had done at the very beginning of the wedding feast.

Then Matholwch and Bendigeidfran began to talk. And Bendigeidfran found Matholwch's conversation lifeless and sad; before this, his conversation had always delighted him. And he supposed that Matholwch was dispirited because he thought his compensation insufficient.

'I tell you,' said Bendigeidfran, 'you're not such a good talker tonight as you were before. And if this is because you think your compensation's not enough, I'll give you as much as you think right. And tomorrow your horses will be paid to you.'

'My lord,' said Matholwch, 'may God bless you.'

'And I'll increase your compensation in this way too,' said Bendigeidfran. 'I'll give you a great cauldron, and the wonder of the cauldron is this: if one of your men should be killed today, throw him into the cauldron; by tomorrow, he'll be as good as ever he was, except that he won't be able to speak.'

Matholwch thanked him for this and no longer felt so heavy-hearted.

The following day Matholwch was paid his horses – that is to say, every trained horse in the court was handed over to him. And then the King was taken to another part of the country, and more horses were given to him there until the payment had been made in full.

And for the second night Bendigeidfran and Matholwch sat down together. 'My lord,' said Matholwch, 'where did the cauldron you gave me come from?'

'It was given to me by a man who had travelled in your country,' said Bendigeidfran. 'And, as far as I know, he got it there.'

'Who was he?' Matholwch asked.

'Llasar the Canny Barterer,' answered Bendigeidfran. 'He came here from Ireland and his wife came with him. They had escaped from an iron house that was set alight while they were inside it. Have you never heard about this?'

'I have heard about it, my lord,' said he, 'and I'll tell you all I know. One day I was hunting in Ireland on a hill above a lake, and it was called the Lake of the Cauldron. And I saw a large man with reddish-yellow hair coming out of the lake with a cauldron on his back. He was an enormous man, with a harsh face; and a woman and her children followed him. And if he was big, his wife was twice his size! And they came towards me and greeted me.

'"Yes," I said, "how are things with you?"

'"This is how things are, my lord," he answered. "This woman – in six weeks' time she's going to have a baby; and this baby will be born a fully-armed warrior."

'I took them to my court to look after them. They stayed with me for a year. During that year there were no complaints from them, but after that they began to grumble. And by the end of the fourth month they were making themselves disliked and unwelcome in the country. They were doing harm, and causing distress, and upsetting gentlefolk. From then on my people pressed me to get rid of them, and they gave me a choice: either my kingdom, or Llasar and his family. I put the matter of what could be done with them to my country's council. They would not go willingly; and they could not be forced to go against their will, because of their huge strength. Because of this, my people decided to build a hall out of iron. And when the hall was ready, they summoned every smith in Ireland, and every man who owned hammer and tongs. And they heaped charcoal as high as the roof of the hall, and then plied Llasar and his wife and children with whatever food and drink they wanted. When it was plain that they were drunk, my people lit the charcoal stacked outside the hall, and began to pump the bellows placed around the house – there was one man for every two bellows. They blew the bellows until the house was white-hot. And then the man and his wife talked together inside the hall. Llasar waited until the iron wall was white-hot and molten. Because the heat was so intense he shoulder-charged the wall and smashed his way out. His wife came out after him. And it was after that, I suppose,' said Matholwch, 'that he came over to you, my lord.'

'It was after that,' said Bendigeidfran, 'that he came here, and gave me this cauldron.'

'My lord, what kind of welcome did you give them?'

'I divided Llasar's family and settled them in every corner of the country. There are a lot of them, and they increase from year to year. They reinforce whatever place they are in, for they make the best warriors, and fashion the best weapons, that were ever seen.'

The two kings went on talking that night for as long as it pleased them, and they enjoyed songs and food. And when they realised they would do better to sleep than to sit there, they went to bed. And when this feast had come to an end, Matholwch set out for Ireland taking Branwen with him. They set out from Abermenai in thirteen ships, and came to Ireland.

In Ireland they were given a great welcome. No nobleman or lady in Ireland came to visit Branwen without her offering them a brooch or a ring or a jewel – the kind of thing very seldom given as a gift. As a result, people sang Branwen's praises; pleasant were her days and she won many friends. Then Branwen became pregnant and, after nine months, gave birth to a son. He was named Gwern. And Gwern was given to foster-parents in the place which was

Branwen's Messenger

acknowledged to be the best in all Ireland for rearing men of high standing.

The following year, there was an outcry in Ireland about the shabby trick that had been played with Matholwch's horses, and the disgrace he had suffered in Wales. His foster-brothers and relatives began to taunt him openly. Soon the whole country was in uproar and Matholwch saw that he would get no peace until his wrong had been avenged. The vengeance taken on Branwen was to expel her from Matholwch's chamber and force her to cook in the court kitchen. The butcher was ordered to come each day and slap her face with his bloodied hands. That is how she was punished.

'Now, my lord,' said his men to Matholwch, 'stop any ship or boat or coracle from going to Wales. And whoever comes here from Wales, throw them into prison. Keep them there in case Bendigeidfran hears rumours about his sister.' And this is exactly what the King did.

Things went on like this for three years until Branwen began to play with a starling that settled on the edge of her kneading-bowl; she taught it to speak and told it what kind of man her brother was. And she taught it to carry a letter describing her punishment and humiliation. She tied this letter to the bird's wing and sent it flying towards Wales.

The bird reached the Island of Britain, and found Bendigeidfran in council at Caer Saint in Arfon. The starling settled on his shoulder and ruffled its feathers. Then the King's followers saw the letter and realised the bird was a tame one. They untied and read the letter. And when he heard it, Bendigeidfran was deeply moved by his sister's account of her punishment. He immediately sent out messengers to gather together the warriors of the island. The King ordered the warriors of one hundred and fifty-four regions to come to him and complained to them himself about his sister's punishment.

Then a council was held. The King and his warriors resolved to go to Ireland and to leave seven men in charge of the Island of the Mighty. And Caradog, son of Brân, was their leader.

So Bendigeidfran and his army sailed for Ireland. Bendigeidfran himself waded through the water for, at that time, the sea was not wide: it was just the width of two rivers, Lli and Archan. And the King walked on towards Ireland, carrying all the harpists on his back.

Matholwch's swineherds were by the sea-shore one day, looking after their pigs, when they saw this wonder. At once they went to Matholwch. 'My lord,' they said, 'greetings to you.'

'God go with you,' said he. 'What news have you?'

'Strange news, my lord. We've seen trees standing out at sea, where we never saw a single tree before.'

'That is strange,' said he. 'Could you see anything else?'

'Yes, my lord,' they answered, 'a great mountain near the trees; a moving mountain! It had a high ridge, and a lake on either side of it. And the trees and the mountain and everything else were moving!'

'Hm!' said he. 'No one here will know about these things unless Branwen does. Ask her.'

The messengers went to Branwen. 'My lady,' they said, 'what do you think these things are?'

'Though I'm not a lady,' said Branwen, 'I know what they are: the men of the Island of the Mighty coming over the sea. They must have heard of my punishment and shame.'

'What are the trees that we saw on the sea?' they asked.

'Masts of ships, and yard-arms,' she answered.

'Oh!' they said. 'And what was the mountain near the trees?'

'My brother Bendigeidfran,' she answered. 'He's wading through the shallows. There's no ship can hold him.'

'What was the high ridge with the lakes on either side of it?'

'Bendigeidfran,' she said, 'glaring at this island. The two lakes and the ridge are his eyes and his nose.'

Then Matholwch and his followers swiftly summoned all the warriors of Ireland and held a council.

'My lord,' said his noblemen, 'there's only one wise thing we can do – retreat over the River Shannon, leaving the river between him and you, and then destroy the bridge. There are lodestones in the river-bed which will drag down any vessel; neither ship nor craft nor raft can get across the water.' And so they retreated across the river and destroyed the bridge.

After a while Bendigeidfran and his fleet reached land near the bank of this river.

'My lord,' said his noblemen to Bendigeidfran, 'you've heard about this strange river: no one can cross it, and there's no bridge over it. How can we get over it?'

'There's nothing for it,' he said, 'but for your leader to be a bridge. I shall be a bridge.'

So Bendigeidfran laid himself across the river, and his warriors crossed over him. As soon as he stood up, messengers came to him and brought him greetings from Matholwch, his kinsman. 'Matholwch,' they said, 'is giving the kingship of Ireland to his son Gwern, your sister's son. He wants to crown him in your presence as compensation for the wrong and insult inflicted on Branwen. Wherever you wish – here or in the Island of the Mighty – make things ready for Matholwch.'

Bridging the Shannon

The Cauldron of Rebirth

'Yes,' said Bendigeidfran. 'Well, if I'm not to have this crown for myself, I must ask my warriors for their opinion of your offer. So first improve it, then I'll say yes or no.'

'We understand,' they said. 'We'll bring you the best offer we can get. Wait until we come back.'

'I'll wait,' he said, 'if you come quickly.'

Away went the messengers and they came to Matholwch. 'My lord,' they said, 'make Bendigeidfran a better offer. He paid little heed to the first one.'

'Well, then,' said Matholwch, 'what's your advice?'

'My lord,' they said, 'there's only one thing to do. There has never been a house large enough to hold Bendigeidfran. Build a house in his honour, a house that will hold him and the men of the Island of the Mighty in one half, and you and your warriors in the other half. You must also give him your crown and do homage to him. Then, because of the honour of having a house that will hold him – a thing he's never had before – he'll make peace with you.'

So the messengers returned to Bendigeidfran with this message. Then the King held a council, and decided to accept Matholwch's offer. And this all came about because of Branwen's advice; she did not want the whole country to be ravaged.

Peace was agreed, and the house built was big and beautiful. But the Irish played a trick on the men of Britain. They hammered a long nail into both sides of every one of the hundred pillars in the house, and hung a skin bag, a 'belly', on every nail, and they hid an armed warrior in every one of these bellies.

Efnisien entered the house in advance of the warriors of the Island of the Mighty and looked around him with blazing eyes and burning anger. Then he saw the bellies hanging on the pillars. 'What's in this belly?' he asked one of the Irishmen.

'Flour, my friend.'

Efnisien prodded the 'flour' until he got hold of a warrior's head. He squeezed it until he felt his fingers sinking through the skull into the brains. Then he turned, put his hand on another belly, and asked, 'And what's in this?'

'Flour,' said the Irishman.

Efnisien fingered every single bag and the heads inside them, so that there was only one man left alive out of the two hundred. He came to this last one and asked, 'What's in this?'

'Flour, my friend,' said the Irishman.

Once again Efnisien felt it until he had found the head, and as he had squeezed the other heads, he squeezed this one too. He could feel a helmet on this warrior's head, but that did not stop him from killing him. Then Efnisien sang:

'In these bellies are all sorts of "flours",
Men savage in war, soldiers too, and warriors;
For battle they're ready, these various sorts of "flours"!'

At this moment, hundreds of people crowded into the house. The men of the Island of Ireland came into the house on one side, and the men of the Island of the Mighty on the other. As soon as they had sat down, there was accord between Bendigeidfran and Matholwch, and the boy Gwern was crowned king.

Then, after arrangements for peace had been completed, Bendigeidfran called the boy to him. From him Gwern passed to Manawydan; and everyone who saw him made a fuss of him. Then Nisien called the boy to him from Manawydan, and he went graciously. 'Why,' said Efnisien, 'does my nephew, my sister's son, not come to me? Even if he were not King of Ireland, I'd be glad to get to know him.'

'Go to him in friendship,' said Bendigeidfran.

The boy went gladly.

'I swear to God,' thought Efnisien, 'I'll be the cause now of a disaster no one here expects.'

Then Efnisien stood up and took the boy by his feet. And before anyone in the hall could move to stop him, he threw the boy headfirst into the blazing fire. When Branwen saw her own child burning she tried to leap from her seat between her two brothers into the fire. But Bendigeidfran held her with one hand and picked up his shield with the other. And then everyone in the house got up. The uproar was the greatest that a crowd ever made in any house as everyone went to his weapons. And while the others reached for their weapons Bendigeidfran held Branwen between his shield and his shoulder.

Then the Irish began to kindle a fire under the cauldron of rebirth, and they threw the bodies of their dead into the cauldron until it was full. The following morning those warriors came out of the cauldron as fit and strong as they had ever been, except that they could not speak.

Efnisien saw there were so many corpses of the men of the Island of the Mighty that there was no room for them anywhere. 'Alas!' he thought. 'I've been the cause of this pile of dead of the Island of the Mighty. And shame on me,' he thought, 'if I do not try to save my people.'

Then Efnisien buried himself amongst the dead bodies of the Irish. And two Irishmen stripped to the waist came and threw him in the cauldron, taking him to be an Irishman. Efnisien stretched himself in the cauldron, he stretched until it broke into four pieces, and his heart broke too because of the strain. It was because of this that the men of the Island of the Mighty gained the victory, such as it was. Only seven men escaped alive, and Bendigeidfran with them – wounded in the foot with a poisoned spear. And these seven men were Pryderi, Manawydan, Glifiau son of Taran, Taliesin, Ynawg, Gruddiau son of Muriel, and Heilyn son of Gwyn the Old. Then Bendigeidfran ordered the seven of them to cut off his head.

'And take the head,' he said, 'and carry it to the White Hill in London, and bury it with its face towards France. And you'll be a long time on the road: you'll stay at Harlech, feasting, for seven years, with the Birds of Rhiannon singing to you. And the head will keep you just as good company as it did when it was between my shoulders. Then you will stay in Gwales, in Penfro, for eighty years. And until you open the door at Gwales which looks towards Aber Henfelen, in Cornwall, you will be able to stay there and the head, none the worse, with you. But from the moment you open that door, you cannot remain there. Go to London then and bury the head. And now, set out for the Island of the Mighty.'

Then Bendigeidfran's head was cut off. And the seven men with the head, taking Branwen as an eighth, set out for the Island of the Mighty.

They reached land at Aber Alaw in Tal Ebolion and sat down to rest. Branwen looked back at Ireland, and at the Island of the Mighty – what she could see of them.

'Ah! Son of God,' she said, 'woe is me that ever I was born! The good of two islands has been destroyed because of me.' Then Branwen gave a great sigh and her heart broke. A four-sided grave was made for her, and she was buried there on the bank of the Alaw.

After that the seven men went on towards Harlech, taking the head with them. And a company of men and women came out to meet them.

'Have you any news?' asked Manawydan.

'Only this,' they replied. 'Caswallon, son of Beli, has conquered the Island of the Mighty and is now King in London.'

'And what happened,' asked the seven, 'to Caradog, son of Brân, and those men left with him on this island?'

'Caswallon surprised and killed six of them. And Caradog's heart broke, for he could see a sword striking his men but did not know who wielded it. Caswallon was wearing a magic cloak, and no one could see him striking the men: all they could see was his sword. And Caswallon did not want to kill Caradog because he was the son of his cousin.'

Then the seven warriors went to Harlech and stayed there. And they started to eat. And as soon as they had started to eat three birds came and began to sing them a song. And every song they had ever heard was unpleasant compared to this singing. The men had to gaze far out over the waves to catch sight of the birds; and yet their singing was so clear that it was as if they were overhead. And they stayed there feasting for seven years.

At the end of the seventh year the seven warriors set out for Gwales in Penfro. A fair and royal palace had been prepared for them there, overlooking the sea; it was a great hall. They went to that hall. They could see two doors open. The third door was shut, and that was the door facing Cornwall.

'Do you see that?' said Manawydan. 'That is the door we are not to open.'

That evening they lacked neither food nor drink nor talk nor song – they were happy together. Despite the great sorrow and suffering they had seen and themselves endured, they had no memory of it or of any grief.

They remained there for eighty years. None of them thought he had ever spent time in a more pleasant or delightful manner. Every year was as happy as the first, and from each other's appearance, none of them could have guessed he had been there for so long. And to have the head with them was no less pleasant than when Bendigeidfran was with them and alive.

But this is what Heilyn, one of the seven, did one day. 'Shame on me,' he said, 'if I don't open the door and find out if what is said about it is true.'

Heilyn opened the door and looked towards Cornwall and Aber Henfelen.

And when he looked all the grief that had ever befallen them, and all the relatives and friends they had lost, and all the evil that had happened to them, were as clear to them as if they had just occurred. And the memory of their lord Bendigeidfran was most painful of all. And from that time they could not remain there, but set out for London taking the head with them. At last they reached London and they buried the head in the White Hill.

And that is how this branch of the Mabinogi ends.

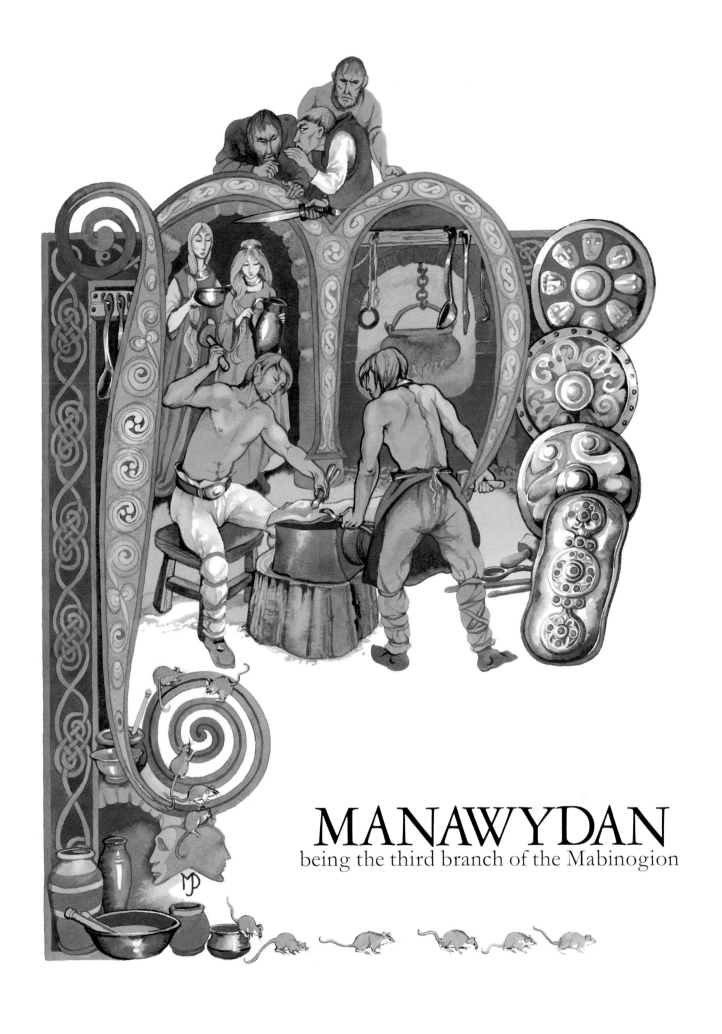

MANAWYDAN
being the third branch of the Mabinogion

MANAWYDAN, SON OF LLŶR

After the seven men in Branwen's story had buried the head of Bendigeidfran in the White Hill in London, with its face looking towards France, Manawydan stared at the town of London and at his friends. He gave a great sigh and became very sad and full of longing.

'O God almighty,' he said, 'woe is me! Everyone has a place to sleep tonight except for me.'

'My lord,' said Pryderi, 'don't be sad. Your cousin is the King of the Island of the Mighty, and though he has done you wrong, you were never one to claim land and territory for yourself. You are a peaceable man.'

'Yes,' he said, 'even though that man is my cousin, it grieves me to see anyone in place of my brother Bendigeidfran. I couldn't be happy in the same house as Caswallon.'

'Will you take advice?' asked Pryderi.

'I need some kind of advice,' said Manawydan. 'What advice do you have for me?'

'The seven regions of Dyfed were left to me,' said Pryderi, 'and my mother, Rhiannon, is there. I shall give Rhiannon to you as your wife, and I shall also give you authority over the seven regions. And though you'll have no land except those seven regions, there are none better. My wife is Cigfa, daughter of Gwyn the Resplendent. And though the kingdom will be in my name, you and Rhiannon can do what you will with it. And if you had ever wanted a kingdom, there are many that are worse than the regions of Dyfed.'

'I don't want any other land, my lord,' said Manawydan. 'May God repay you for being such a good friend.'

'I shall be as good a friend to you as I can be,' said Pryderi, 'if you want that.'

'Indeed, I do, my friend,' said he. 'And I will come with you to meet Rhiannon and to see the land.'

'You're doing the right thing,' said Pryderi. 'I don't think you'll ever have heard a woman make better conversation. And when she was at her best there was no woman more beautiful than she; and even now you will not be disappointed in her beauty.'

So they went their way and at last they came to Dyfed. And a feast had been prepared for them in Arberth by Rhiannon and Cigfa.

And they sat down together and Manawydan and Rhiannon began to talk. And while they were talking Manawydan began to feel affection for her and to think admiringly that he had never seen a more beautiful woman.

'Pryderi,' said Manawydan, 'I'll agree to what you said.'

'What was that?' asked Rhiannon.

'My lady,' said Pryderi, 'I have given you to be Manawydan's wife.'

'I'll agree to that gladly,' said Rhiannon.

'I'm glad of that,' said Manawydan. 'And may God repay you, Pryderi, for being such a good friend.'

Before the end of that feast they were married.

'Finish what is left of the feast,' said Pryderi, 'and I will go to pay homage to Caswallon, son of Beli, in England.'

'My lord,' said Rhiannon, 'Caswallon is in Kent, and you can continue the feast until he comes nearer.'

'If that's so,' said Pryderi, 'we'll wait.'

They finished the feast and began to ride through Dyfed, and to hunt and enjoy themselves.

And as they travelled through the country, they thought they had never seen a more pleasant place to live in, nor better land for hunting, nor a land with more honey and fish. And what with all this, such a friendship grew up between the four of them that none wished to be without the others by day or by night.

In the meantime, Pryderi went to pay homage to Caswallon at Oxford. He was received with joy, and with gratitude for his homage. And after he had returned, Pryderi and Manawydan feasted together and spent their time in delight.

And they began a feast in Arberth because that was the principal court and because every important celebration began there. And after the first sitting that evening, while the servants were eating, the four friends went walking. Accompanied by a crowd of people, they went to the Throne of Arberth. And while they were sitting there they heard a noise, and because of that noise a thick mist fell so that they could not see each other. And after the mist the whole place was filled with light. And when they looked in the direction where the flocks and herds of animals and the houses had been, they could not see anything at all. They could see no animal, no smoke, no fire, no man, not a single house (apart from the court buildings – and those were empty and desolate, with no one in them). And the entire company – apart from the four of them – had disappeared without trace.

'O Lord God,' said Manawydan, 'where are the people of the court and our companions? Let's go to look for them.'

They came to the court: not a soul was there. They went to the sleeping chambers: not a soul was to be seen. In the wine cellar, in the kitchen – nothing but desolation.

After a while the four of them began to eat the food of the feast, and to hunt and enjoy themselves. And they began to travel through the kingdom to see if any house or habitation remained: they saw nothing but wild animals. And after they had finished their feast, and all the food that had been prepared, they began to hunt for food, and to eat fish, and the honey of swarms of wild bees. For one year, and a second, they were well satisfied with this, but at last they grew tired of it.

'Believe me,' said Manawydan, 'we can't live like this. We must go to England so that we can earn a living.'

And they went towards England, and came to Hereford and began to make saddles. Manawydan began to make pommels and to colour them, as he had learned from Llasar the Canny Barterer, with blue enamel. Whilst saddle-work of this kind was available from Manawydan, no one would buy a pommel or a saddle from any other saddler throughout Hereford. All the saddlers realised they were losing their livelihood and that no one would buy from them except when they could not buy from Manawydan. At this they met and agreed to kill Manawydan and his friend. But Manawydan and Pryderi were warned about this plot and advised to leave the town.

'As God is my witness,' said Pryderi, 'I don't want us to leave this town, I want to kill these bondsmen.'

'No,' said Manawydan. 'If we were to fight them, we would get ourselves a bad name and be thrown into prison. It's better for us to go to another town to earn our living.'

And then the four of them went to another place.

'What craft,' asked Pryderi, 'shall we practise here?'

'We'll make shields,' said Manawydan.

'Do we know anything about that?' asked Pryderi.

'We'll try it,' he said.

And they began to make shields, and they coloured them with the blue enamel they had put on the saddles.

This work so prospered that no one in the whole town would buy a shield elsewhere unless he was unable to buy one from them. They worked quickly and made many shields. Things went on in this way until their fellow townsmen grew angry with them and agreed to kill them. But Manawydan and Pryderi were warned; they heard a rumour that some men intended to kill them.

'Pryderi,' said Manawydan, 'these men are after our blood.'

'We need not suffer at the hands of these bondsmen,' said Pryderi. 'We'll attack them and kill them.'

The Enchantment of Dyfed

'No, we won't,' said Manawydan. 'Caswallon and his men would hear about that, and that would be the end of us. We'll go to another town.'

They came to another town.

'What craft shall we practise?' asked Manawydan.

'Whatever craft you like out of those we know,' said Pryderi.

'We'll try shoemaking,' he said. 'Shoemakers won't have the heart to fight us or stop us.'

'I know nothing about the craft,' said Pryderi.

'I do,' said Manawydan, 'and I'll teach you to stitch. And we won't bother to dress the leather but buy it ready-dressed, and make our shoes with that.'

Manawaydan began to buy Spanish leather, the finest cordwain that he could find in the town. He would buy no other leather – except for the soles. And he began to spend some time with the best goldsmith in the town, and had buckles fashioned for the shoes. And he carefully watched the way the goldsmith worked until he had mastered his craft.

For as long as a shoe of any kind was to be had from Manawydan, no one would buy any from the other shoemakers in the town. And the shoemakers realised that things were going badly for them because, while Manawydan cut the leather, Pryderi stitched it. The shoemakers met to discuss what to do, and they agreed to kill Manawydan and Pryderi.

'Pryderi,' said Manawydan, 'these men intend to kill us.'

'Why should we suffer at the hands of these thieving bondsmen,' asked Pryderi, 'instead of killing them all?'

'No,' said Manawydan, 'we won't fight them, and we won't stay in England any longer. We'll go to Dyfed and survey the kingdom.'

At last they came to Dyfed and went to Arberth. And they kindled a fire and began to eat and to hunt; they spent a month in this way. Then they gathered their hounds and went hunting; and they lived in this way for a year.

One morning Manawydan and Pryderi got up to go hunting, and made their hounds ready, and went out of the court. Some of the hounds ran ahead of them and went into a little copse nearby. And no sooner had they gone into the copse than they beat a hasty retreat with their hair standing on end, and ran back to the men. 'We'll go nearer to the copse,' said Pryderi, 'to see what is in it.'

They came nearer to the copse. And when they approached it, a shining white wild boar rushed out of it. The men urged the hounds to close on the boar. And the boar left the copse and retreated some way from the men. And if the men kept their distance, the boar would turn and face the hounds, fearless before them: and when the men came near, the boar would retreat again and not stand his ground.

The Boar Hunt

And they followed the boar until they saw a huge and lofty fort, newly built; and that was in a place where they had never seen a stone or any building. The boar went quickly into the fort, followed by the hounds. And after the boar and the hounds had gone into the fort, the men began to marvel at the sight of the fort in a place where they had never seen any building before. And from the top of the mound they looked, and listened for the hounds. But, though they stayed there, they heard no sound of the hounds nor saw any sign of them.

'My lord,' said Pryderi, 'I'll go into the fort to see if the hounds are there.'

'Indeed,' said Manawydan, 'I don't think that is a good idea. We've never seen this fort before. And if you take my advice, you will not go into it. Whoever has cast a spell on this land has also caused this fort to appear here.'

'Believe me,' said Pryderi, 'I'm not going to lose my pack of hounds.'

Despite all Manawydan's advice, Pryderi insisted on going towards the fort.

When he came to it, there was not a man nor beast inside it, not the boar, nor the hounds, nor a house, nor any place to live in. Near the middle of the grounds of the fort, Pryderi could see a well with marble work around it. And just by the well he could see a golden cauldron held by four chains and hanging above a marble slab. And the chains went up to the sky, and he could see no end to them. Pryderi began to marvel at the beauty of the gold and the splendid workmanship of the cauldron. He came to the cauldron and took hold of it. And as soon as he held the cauldron, his hands stuck fast to it, and his feet stuck to the place where he was standing, and he lost his voice so that he could not utter a word. That is how he stood there.

Manawydan waited for him almost until the end of the day. And late in the afternoon, when he was certain he would hear nothing of Pryderi or his hounds, he went back to the court. When he returned, Rhiannon looked at him.

'Where,' she said, 'is your friend and your hounds?'

'This,' he said, 'is my story . . .' And he told it all.

'Indeed,' said Rhiannon, 'you've been a bad friend and you've lost a good friend.'

And with that, out she went. She went in the direction of the fort, as Manawydan had described it.

Rhiannon saw the gate of the fort open, and in she went. As soon as she came there, she saw Pryderi holding on to the cauldron, and came to him. 'Oh! My lord,' she said, 'what are you doing?'

And Rhiannon grasped the cauldron like Pryderi. As soon as she did so, her hands stuck fast to it and her feet stuck fast to the marble slab, so that she could not utter a word. And then, as soon as it was night, there was a great

A Land Rich in Fish

noise about them, and a mist fell, and the fort vanished, and they inside it.

When Cigfa, Pryderi's wife, saw there was no one in the court but herself and Manawydan she began to weep as if she were about to die. Then Manawydan looked at her.

'Indeed,' he said, 'you're mistaken if you're weeping because you're afraid of me. As God's your witness, you've never seen a more faithful friend than I. Don't be afraid,' he said. 'Indeed, you'll have my friendship while we are in this trouble and misery.'

'May God repay you,' she said. 'I knew that I could trust you.'

And then, because of this, the young woman began to be spirited and more confident.

'Indeed, dear friend,' said Manawydan, 'this is not a proper place for us to stay. We've lost our hounds and we cannot find food. We'll make for England – it's much easier to find food there.'

'Gladly, my lord,' said Cigfa.

And they travelled together towards England.

'My lord,' she said, 'whatever craft you mean to practise, make sure it's worthy of your station.'

'I shall take up no craft but that of a shoemaker, as I did before,' Manawydan said.

'My lord,' she said, 'that is not a suitable craft for so skilled and accomplished a man as you.'

'That's the one I'm going to practise,' he said.

And Manawydan began to practise his craft and made his work of the finest cordwain he could find in the town. And as he and Pryderi had done before in the other place, he began to make gold buckles for the shoes, until the work of all the shoemakers in the town looked shabby and skimpy by comparison. And while any sort of shoe was to be had from him, no one would buy anything from anyone else.

Manawydan spent a year in this way, until the shoemakers were jealous and envious of him, and until warnings and whisperings reached him that they had agreed to kill him.

'My lord,' said Cigfa, 'why should we endure this at the hands of these bondsmen?'

'No,' he said, 'we'll go to Dyfed in spite of all this.'

They set out for Dyfed. And what Manawydan did was to carry a measure of wheat with him. And he made for Arberth, and remained there. Nothing was more pleasant to him than to see Arberth and the land where he and Pryderi had gone hunting, and Rhiannon with them.

Then Manawydan began to accustom himself to catching fish and hunting animals there. And after that he began to till the land; and after that to sow a

Manawydan the Shoemaker

field, and a second, and a third. The wheat showed up through the earth splendidly, and Manawydan's three fields flourished equally well, so that no one had ever seen finer wheat. Thus he passed the year, one season after the other.

Harvest time came. He went to look at one of his fields. It was ripe.

'I'll come and reap it tomorrow,' he said. And he returned to Arberth that night.

Next day at dawn, Manawydan set out to reap the field. When he arrived, there was nothing but bare stalks there, every ear of wheat had been snapped off, every stalk broken. And the ears of wheat had all been carried off, leaving the stalks there completely bare.

He wondered greatly at this, and went to look at another field. The wheat there was fine and ripe.

'Indeed,' he said, 'I'll come and reap this tomorrow.'

On the following day Manawydan came, intent upon reaping it. But when he reached it, there was nothing there but bare stalks.

'O Lord God,' he said, 'who is bent upon ruining me? . . . Ah! I know – he who began my ruin is going to finish his work! And it's he who has ruined this land as well as ruining me.'

Manawydan came to look at the third field. When he did so, no one had ever seen finer wheat, and it was fine and ripe.

'Shame upon me,' he said, 'if I don't keep watch tonight. Whatever stole the other wheat will come to steal this wheat too. And I shall find out what it is.'

Manawydan took his weapons and prepared to keep watch over the field. He told all this to Cigfa.

'Yes,' she said, 'what's in your mind?'

'I'll keep watch over the field tonight,' he said.

And off he went to watch. And at midnight, as he was keeping watch in this way, there was the greatest noise in the world. Manawydan looked. There was an enormous horde of mice! It was impossible to reckon their number or quantity! But Manawydan was still none the wiser until the mice made for his field, and every mouse climbed a stalk, bent it under its weight, broke the ear of wheat and then made off with it, leaving the stalk behind. And it did not seem as if there were a single stalk without a mouse on it. And the mice were carrying away the wheat! Then, in wrath and anger, Manawydan rushed in amongst the mice. And he could no more keep his eye on a single mouse than on one gnat or one bird in the air. But he could see one mouse that was so heavy that he imagined it could not move quickly. He chased it and caught it. He put it in his glove and tied the mouth of the glove with string to keep it inside, and then made for the court.

Manawydan arrived at the court where Cigfa was, and kindled a fire. And he hung the glove by its string on a peg.

'What's in there, my lord?' asked Cigfa.

'A thief,' he said, 'that I found stealing from me.'

'What kind of a thief, my lord, could you put in your glove?' she asked.

'Here's the whole story,' he said, and told her how his fields had been destroyed and ruined, and how the mice had come to the last field whilst he was keeping watch there.

'And one of them was heavy, and I caught it, and that's the one in the glove. And I'll hang it tomorrow. And as God's my witness, if I'd caught all of them, I'd have hanged them all.'

'My lord,' she said, 'that's not surprising . . . and yet it's scarcely proper to see a man of your rank and dignity hanging a creature like that. If you were to do right, you wouldn't harm the creature but let it go.'

'Shame upon me,' he said, 'I would hang them all if only I could catch them! And the one that I've caught – it will hang.'

'Fine, my lord,' she said. 'I've no reason at all to help that creature – except to save you from getting a bad name. Do as you will, my lord.'

'If I knew of any reason in the world why you should want to help that creature,' he said, 'I would follow your advice; but since I know of no such reason, my lady, I intend to destroy it.'

'Do that, gladly,' she said.

And then Manawydan made for the Throne of Arberth, and he took the mouse with him. He thrust two forked sticks into the highest part of the mound. And as he did so, he could see a scholar coming towards him, wearing poor threadbare old clothes. And it was seven years since Manawydan had seen either man or beast in Dyfed, apart from his friends.

'My lord,' said the scholar, 'good day to you!'

'God prosper you! And welcome to you!' said Manawydan. Then he asked, 'Where do you come from, scholar?'

'I come from England, my lord. I've been singing there,' he replied. 'And why do you ask, my lord?' he enquired.

'Before I saw you, I'd not seen anyone here,' said he, 'for seven years, apart from myself and three companions who are now separated.'

'Indeed, my lord,' said he. 'I'm making my way through this kingdom to my own country. And what kind of work are you doing, my lord?'

'Hanging a thief I caught stealing from me,' he said.

'What thief, my lord?' he asked. 'I see nothing but a creature in your hand, a creature like a mouse; and it ill becomes a man of your rank and dignity to have anything to do with a creature like that. Let it go.'

'I won't, as God is my witness,' said he. 'I caught it stealing, and I shall deal with it according to the law for thieves – I shall hang it.'

'My lord,' he said, 'rather than see a nobleman such as yourself stoop to such work, I'll give you this pound – I earned it by begging! – if you release this creature.'

'No, I won't, as God's my witness; I will not sell it.'

'Do as you will, my lord,' said he. 'If it were not so shameful to see a man of your rank and dignity bothering with a creature like that, it would not concern me.'

And away went the scholar.

As Manawydan was placing the cross-beam in the forks of the scaffold, a priest came towards him on a fine horse.

'My lord, good day to you,' he said.

'God prosper you!' said Manawydan. 'Give me your blessing.'

'May God bless you,' said the priest. 'And what kind of work are you doing, my lord?'

'Hanging a thief I caught stealing from me,' he answered.

'What thief, my lord?' he asked.

'A creature,' he said, 'in the form of a mouse. It stole from me; and I shall give it the death of a thief.'

'My lord, rather than see you bother yourself with that creature, I'll buy it. Let it go.'

'I swear to God, I will not sell it nor set it free.'

'It's true, my lord, that it's worthless; but rather than see you sully yourself with the creature, I'll give you three pounds if you let it go.'

'As God's my witness,' he said, 'I want nothing except what it deserves – to be hanged.'

'Very well, my lord, do as you will.'

And away went the priest.

And Manawydan put the string noose about the neck of the mouse. And as he was lifting it he saw approaching a bishop's retinue and baggage; and the bishop himself was coming towards him.

Manawydan stayed his hand.

'My lord bishop,' he said, 'give me your blessing.'

'May God bless you,' he said. 'What kind of work are you doing?'

'Hanging a thief I caught stealing from me,' said Manawydan.

'Is it not a mouse,' he said, 'that I see in your hand?'

'Yes,' he said, 'a thief.'

'Well,' said the bishop, 'since I've arrived as that creature is about to be destroyed, I'll buy it from you. I'll give you seven pounds for it. Rather than see a nobleman such as yourself destroy so useless a creature, let it go, and you will have the money.'

'No, I won't, as God's my witness,' said he.

'Since you won't let it go for that sum, I'll give you twenty-four pounds in cash – if you let it go.'

'No, I won't let it go, I swear to God, not even for double that amount,' he said.

'Since you won't let it go for that sum,' said the bishop, 'I'll give you as many horses as you see in this meadow, together with the seven packs carried by the seven horses.'

'No, I won't settle for that, as God's my witness,' he said.

'Since you don't want that, name your price for the mouse.'

'I shall,' he said. 'The release of Rhiannon and Pryderi.'

'You can have that.'

'No, I won't settle for that, as God's my witness.'

'What do you want?'

'The removal of the spell and the enchantment from the seven regions of Dyfed.'

'You can have that too – if you will let the mouse go.'

'No, I won't, as God's my witness,' said Manawydan. 'I must know who the mouse is.'

'She is my wife,' said the bishop, 'and if she were not my wife, I would not want to free her.'

'For what purpose did she come to me?'

'To steal,' said the bishop. 'I am Llwyd, son of Cilcoed, and it is I who cast the spell on the seven regions of Dyfed. And I cast the spell to avenge the wrong done to my friend, Gwawl, son of Clud. And I took vengeance on Pryderi because badger-in-the-bag was played with Gwawl, son of Clud – it was Pwyll, King of the Other World, who unwisely did that in the court of Hefeydd the Old. And when they heard you were living in Pwyll's realm, my soldiers came to me and asked to be changed into mice to destroy your fields of wheat.

'On the first night, it was only my soldiers who came. They came the second night too. And it was they who destroyed the two fields. On the third night, my wife and the ladies of the court came to me and asked me to change them into mice too; and I did that. And my wife was pregnant; and were she not pregnant, you would not have caught her. But since things did not turn out like that, and she was caught, I'll give you Rhiannon and Pryderi and I'll rid Dyfed of the spell and the enchantment. And now I've told you who she is, release her.'

'No, I won't, as God's my witness,' said Manawydan.

'What do you want?' he asked.

'This,' said Manawydan, 'is what I want: that there will not be any spell on the seven regions of Dyfed, and that no spell will ever be cast on them.'

'You can have that,' he said, 'but let her go.'

'No, I won't, as God's my witness,' said Manawydan.

'What do you want?' he asked.

'This,' said Manawydan, 'is what I want: that vengeance will never be taken on Pryderi or on Rhiannon or on me because of all this.'

'You can have all that. And indeed, it is good that you have made this demand,' he said. 'Had you not done so,' he said, 'great harm would have come upon you.'

'Yes,' said Manawydan, 'that is why I made it.'

'But now release my wife.'

'No, I won't, as God's my witness, until I see Pryderi and Rhiannon free and at my side.'

'Look, here they come!' he said.

At that, Pryderi and Rhiannon appeared. Manawydan got up to meet them, and they sat down together.

'Ah! good sir, release my wife for me now, for you have been granted everything you demanded.'

'I will release her, gladly,' he said.

And he set her free, and Llwyd, son of Cilcoed, struck her with his magic wand and changed her back into the most beautiful young woman that anyone had ever seen.

The Bargain with the Bishop

'Look at the land all around you,' said Llwyd, 'and you'll see all the houses and all the dwellings as they were at their best.'

And then Manawydan stood up and looked. And when he looked, he could see the whole kingdom with people living in it, complete with all its herds and all its houses.

And that is how this branch of the Mabinogi ends.

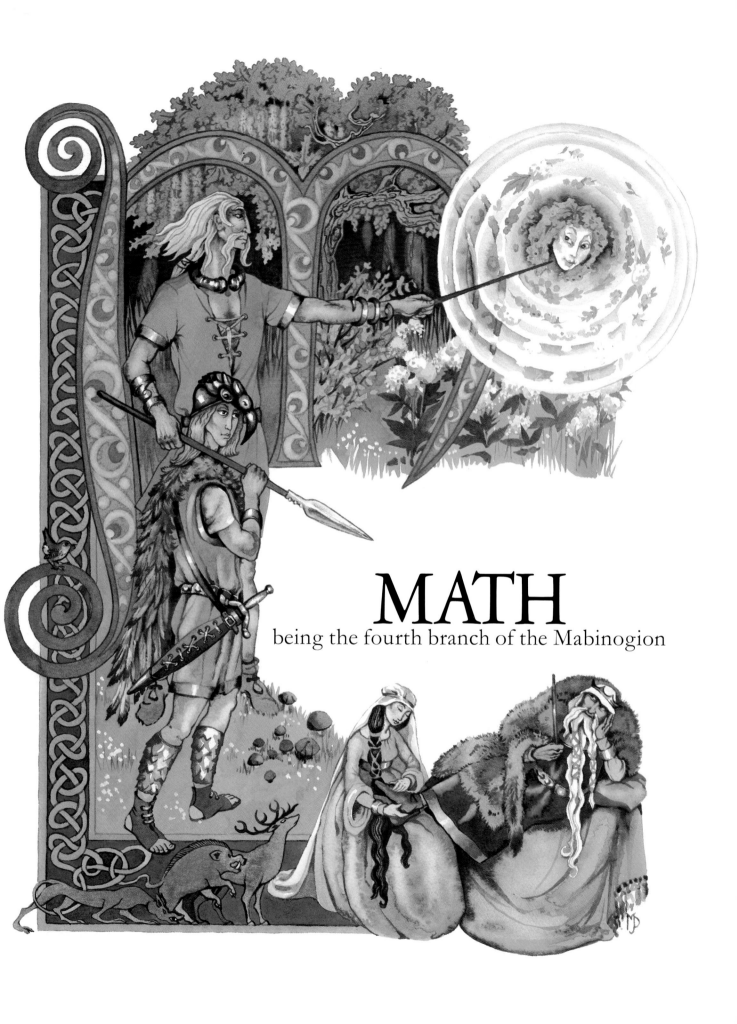

MATH
being the fourth branch of the Mabinogion

MATH, SON OF MATHONWY

Math, son of Mathonwy, was lord of Gwynedd, and Pryderi, son of Pwyll, was lord of Dyfed and other regions in the south. And at this time the life of Math, son of Mathonwy, depended on a very strange circumstance: unless he was fighting in the fury of battle, he had to rest his feet on a maiden's lap. And his maiden was Goewin, daughter of Pebin. No one knew of a fairer maiden; she was the fairest of her time.

And Math spent his time at Caer Dathl in Arfon. And no one was allowed to go on court visits through the land except for Math's nephews, the sons of his sister, Gilfaethwy and Gwydion. The soldiers of the court used to accompany them as they travelled through the land on behalf of Math.

And Goewin remained with Math all the time. Gilfaethwy fell in love with her so that he did not know what to do about it. He lost his colour and his brightness and grew thin because of his love for her, so that he was hard to recognize.

And one day Gwydion, his brother, looked closely at him.

'Well, then!' said Gilfaethwy. 'What do you see wrong with me?'

'I see you losing your colour and your brightness,' said Gwydion. 'What has happened to you?'

'My lord and brother,' he said, 'it's no use my saying a word to anyone about what has happened to me.'

'Why so, lad?' he asked.

'You know,' he said, 'about Math's magic power: if it's possible for the wind to pick up what one man whispers to another, then Math will come to know of it.'

'Yes,' said Gwydion, 'say no more, I know what's on your mind – you're in love with Goewin.'

When Gilfaethwy realised that his brother knew his feelings, he gave the greatest sigh in the world.

'Don't sigh, lad,' said Gwydion, 'that will do no good. Since we cannot change things without some trick,' he said, 'I'll get the soldiers of Gwynedd and Powys to muster for war, so that Math will have to go to fight. Then the maiden will be yours. Be of good cheer! I'll arrange things.'

After this, they went to Math, son of Mathonwy.

'My lord,' said Gwydion, 'I've heard that some creatures that have never before been seen on this island, have come to the south.'

'What are they called?' asked Math.

'Pigs, my lord.'

'What kind of animals are they?'

'Small animals, and their meat is better than that of cows.'

'Who owns them?'

'Pryderi, son of Pwyll. They were sent to him by Arawn, King of the Other World.'

'Indeed,' said Math. 'How may we get them from him?'

'I will go as one of twelve disguised as poets, my lord, to seek these pigs.'

'He may refuse you,' said Math.

'My plan is not a bad one,' said Gwydion. 'I won't come back without the pigs.'

'Go on your way, gladly,' said Math.

Gwydion and Gilfaethwy and ten men with them went to Cardigan, to a place now called Rhuddlan Teifi – Pryderi had a court there. And they came to the court disguised as poets. They were warmly welcomed. And Gwydion was seated next to Pryderi that night.

'You know,' said Pryderi, 'we would like to hear stories told by some of those young men over there.'

'Our custom, my lord,' said Gwydion, 'is that on the first night we come to visit a great man, the chief poet tells a story. I shall gladly tell a tale.'

And Gwydion was the best story-teller in the world. And that night he entertained the court with pleasant conversation and stories, until he was everyone's favourite in the court, and it was a delight for Pryderi to talk with him.

And at the end of it all, Gwydion said, 'My lord, can anyone carry out my errand better than I myself?'

'No,' said Pryderi, 'you have a marvellous tongue.'

'This is my errand, my lord: to try to get from you the animals that were sent to you from the Other World.'

'Ah, well,' he said, 'that would be the easiest thing in the world to do except for the agreement between me and my people about them. That is, they are not to leave this kingdom until they breed twice their own number.'

'My lord,' said Gwydion, 'I can release you from that agreement like this: don't give me the pigs tonight, but don't refuse to give them either. Tomorrow, I'll show you things I'll exchange for them.'

And that night, Gwydion and his friends went to their lodging with the matter undecided.

'Ah, men,' said Gwydion, 'we'll not get these pigs by asking for them.'

'Well,' they said, 'how can we get them then?'

'I'll arrange things so that we get them,' said Gwydion.

And then he devoted himself to his spells and showed his magic powers.

And by his magic he conjured out of toadstools twelve horses, and twelve black hounds with white chests. And he conjured twelve collars, and twelve leashes: and whoever saw these things would certainly have thought that they were made of gold. He conjured twelve saddles for the horses, and the parts that should have been of iron were made entirely of gold; and so were the bridles.

And Gwydion came to Pryderi with the horses and dogs.

'Good day to you, my lord,' he said.

'May God prosper you,' said Pryderi, 'and welcome to you.'

'My lord,' said he, 'here is a way to release you from what you said about the pigs last night, that you could not give them: you can exchange them for something better. I'll give you these twelve horses with their saddles and bridles, just as they are; and these twelve hounds with their leashes and collars, just as you see them. And these twelve gold shields you see there.'

'Well, yes,' said Pryderi, 'we'll take counsel about it.'

And the council decided that the pigs be given to Gwydion and the horses and dogs and shields be accepted in exchange.

And then Gwydion and his friends were given permission to go, and they started on their journey with the pigs.

'My good friends,' said Gwydion, 'we must travel quickly. This spell will last for one day only.'

And that night they and the pigs travelled as far as the uplands of Ceredigion – to the place that is called Mochdref, meaning 'Pig Town', to this day. And the following day they went on their way and came over Elenid. And that night, and the night after in Powys, and the night after in Rhos, they stayed in places which are still called 'Pig Town'.

'Ah, men,' said Gwydion, 'we'll make for the most mighty stronghold of Gwynedd with these animals. They're coming after us in hosts.'

And they made for the highest town in Arllechwedd and made a sty there, a *crau*, for the pigs. And for that reason the name Creuwrion was given to the town. And then, after making a sty for the pigs, they went to Math in Caer Dathl.

When they arrived there the soldiers of the kingdom were being mustered.

'What news is there?' asked Gwydion.

'Pryderi is mustering the soldiers of twenty-one regions with which to pursue you,' they said. 'It's strange how slowly you travelled.'

'Where are the animals you went to fetch?' asked Math.

'A sty has been made for them in the region over there,' said Gwydion.

At that, they heard trumpets and the soldiers of the kingdom mustering. Then they put on their armour and travelled until they were in Pennardd, in Arfon.

That night Gwydion and Gilfaethwy, his brother, went back to Caer Dathl.

Gwydion the Magician

And Gilfaethwy slept with Goewin in Math's bed, and the maidservants were roughly handled and thrown out of their quarters. This shame befell Goewin that night completely against her will.

When the two brothers saw day dawning they made for the place where Math and his soldiers were. When they arrived those men were about to take counsel about the best place to wait for Pryderi and the men of the south, and the two of them came into that council. They decided to wait in the mighty stronghold of Gwynedd, in Arfon, and that night they stayed in the middle of the two districts, Maenor Pennardd and Maenor Coed Alun.

Pryderi attacked them there. A battle was fought and a great number of men on both sides were killed, and the men of the south were forced to retreat. And the place they retreated to is called Nant Call. The men of Gwynedd pursued them there. And a terrifying slaughter took place. Then the men of the south retreated again as far as Dôl Benmaen. And there they met and attempted to make peace, and Pryderi gave some of his men as hostages, to guarantee the truce. And those given as hostages were Gwrgi Gwastra and twenty-three sons of noblemen.

Then, under the conditions of the truce, the men of the south were given safe conduct as far as the Great Strand. But as they were arriving at the Yellow Ford it was impossible to restrain the foot-soldiers from shooting at each other. Pryderi sent messages to order the two sides to desist, and to ask that the matter be left between him and Gwydion, son of Dôn, since he was the cause of the trouble. The messengers came to Math.

'Yes,' said Math, 'as God's my witness, I'm willing for Gwydion to fight if he agrees to it. But I will not compel anyone to fight. We'll do what we can to avoid battle.'

'Truly,' said the messengers, 'Pryderi says it's only fair for the man who wronged him to fight against him, and to leave the two armies out of it.'

'As God's my witness,' said Gwydion, 'I'll not leave the men of Gwynedd to fight on my behalf when I'm given the chance to fight against Pryderi on my own. I shall go against him gladly.'

And this reply was taken to Pryderi.

'Good,' said Pryderi, 'I'll not ask anyone to win my redress for me; I'll fight him myself.'

The two men, Pryderi and Gwydion, were placed apart; and then they were armed; and they fought. And by dint of the greatness of his strength and bravery, and the power of magic and enchantment, Gwydion won and Pryderi was killed. And he was buried in Maen Tyfiawg above the Yellow Ford, and his grave is still there.

The men of the south travelled towards their kingdom chanting their lamentations. It was no wonder: they had lost their lord and many of their best men, and their horses, and the greater part of their arms.

But as for the men of Gwynedd, they went back home with joy and exultation.

'My lord,' said Gwydion to Math, 'shouldn't we release their noblemen to the men of the south – those they gave us as hostages to keep the peace? We ought not to keep them prisoners.'

'Let them be set free, then,' said Math.

And Gwrgi Gwastra and the other hostages were allowed to go after the men of the south.

Then Math made for Caer Dathl. And Gilfaethwy and the soldiers of the court who had been with him, travelled around Gwynedd, without returning to the court. And Math went to his chamber and ordered a place to be made ready so that he could put his feet on his maiden's lap.

'My lord,' said Goewin, 'you'll have to find someone else to take my place at your feet. I'm no longer a maiden.'

'What is the meaning of this?' asked Math.

'I was attacked, my lord, and that openly. And I was not silent about it – there was no one in the court who didn't know it. And those who came, my lord, were your nephews, the sons of your sister, Gwydion and Gilfaethwy. They ravished me and brought shame on you, and that in your own chamber and in your own bed.'

'Indeed,' said he, 'I'll do as much as I can for you. I'll seek redress for you and for myself. And I shall marry you,' he said, 'and give you authority over my kingdom.'

During this time, neither Gwydion nor Gilfaethwy came near the court. They slept here and there on their circuit of the kingdom until a ban was issued that denied them all food and drink. At first they did not come near Math. But, after a while, they came to him.

'My lord,' they said, 'good day to you.'

'So!' he said. 'Have you come here to make amends to me?'

'My lord, do as you will with us.'

'If it were my will, I would not have lost as many men and arms as I have lost. You two cannot make amends to me for the shame you've brought upon me, not to mention amends for the death of Pryderi. But since you've placed yourselves under my authority, I shall begin to punish you.'

And then Math took his magic wand and struck Gilfaethwy so that he became a large hind. And he caught Gwydion quickly too – although he wanted to escape, he could not. Math struck him, too, with the same wand and turned him into a stag.

'Since you like to be together, you can live together and become male and female together, and you'll have the same nature as the wild beasts in whose shapes you are. In the season these animals give birth to their young, you too will give birth. And, a year from today, come here to me.'

A year to the day Math heard a noise under the wall of his chamber, and the barking of the court dogs besides.

'Have a look,' said Math to one of his servants, 'at what's outside.'

'My lord,' the servant said, 'I have looked. There's a stag and a hind, and a fawn with them.'

At that, Math got up and went out. And when he came out, he saw three animals, a stag and a hind and a strong fawn. And what he did was to raise his magic wand.

'The one of you who was a hind last year must be a wild boar this year. And the one of you who was a stag last year must be a wild sow this year.'

And with that he struck them with the magic wand.

'And this fawn,' he said, 'now changed into a boy, I will take him and put him to be fostered and baptised.' And he was named Hyddwn, which means 'the Noble Stag'. 'And you,' he said, 'away with you! One of you will be a wild boar, and the other a wild sow. And you'll have the same nature as wild pigs have. And, a year from today, be here under the wall and your little piglet with you.'

In a year's time, they could hear the noise of dogs barking under the wall of the chamber and, moreover, the noise of the people of the court gathering together. At that, Math got up and went out. And when he came out he could see three animals – a wild boar, a wild sow, and a sturdy piglet with them. And the little pig was large for its age.

'So!' said Math. 'I shall take this one myself and have him baptised.' And he struck it with the magic wand, and changed it into a handsome auburn-haired boy. And he was named Hychdwn, 'the Noble Boar'. 'As for you,' said Math to Gwydion and Gilfaethwy, 'the one who was a wild boar last year is to be a wolf bitch this year. And the one who was a wild sow last year is to be a wolf this year.'

And at that he struck them with the magic wand so that they became a wolf and a wolf bitch.

'And you'll have the same nature as the animals in whose shape you are. And be here, a year from now, beneath this wall.'

A year to the day, Math heard people gathering together and heard barking beneath the chamber wall. He came out. And when he came he saw there a wolf and a wolf bitch, and a sturdy wolf cub with them.

'I shall take this one,' he said, 'and have him baptised. And his name is ready for him: Bleiddwn, "the Noble Wolf". You have three sons now:

> 'False Gilfaethwy has three sons,
> And they are loyal champions:
> Bleiddwn, Hyddwn, Hychdwn the Tall.'

At that, Math struck the two brothers with the magic wand so that they were men again. 'Men,' he said, 'if you did me wrong, you've been punished enough, and shamed by having these children. Let a bath be prepared for these men, let their hair be washed and let them be made presentable.'

And that was done.

After they had been made ready, Gwydion and Gilfaethwy came to Math.

'Men,' he said, 'you have earned your peace, and we shall be friends. Give me your advice as to which maiden I ought to look for.'

'My lord,' said Gwydion, son of Dôn, 'it is easy to advise you: Arianrhod, daughter of Dôn, your niece, your sister's daughter.'

And she was brought to him. She came in.

'Ah! maiden,' said Math, 'do you truly deserve that name?'

'I know nothing to the contrary,' she said.

Then he took his magic wand and bent it. 'Step over this,' he told her, 'and if you are a maiden, I shall know.'

Then Arianrhod stepped over the magic wand. And as she did so, she dropped a large baby boy with yellow hair. And the boy gave a loud cry. At this cry, she made for the door and, as she did so, she dropped something else, quite small. Before anyone could get a second look at it, Gwydion took it, put a cover of silk over it and hid it. And he hid it in a small chest at the foot of his bed.

'Indeed,' said Math, looking at the sturdy yellow-haired boy, 'I shall have this one baptised. And I shall name him Dylan, "the Sea".' So the boy was baptised. And as soon as he was baptised he made for the sea. And no sooner did he reach the water's edge than the sea's nature came upon him and he swam as well as the finest fish. And because of that, he was called Dylan, son of the Wave. No wave ever broke under him.

One day, while Gwydion was in bed and waking up, he heard a cry from the chest at his feet. Though it was not a loud cry, it was loud enough for him to hear it. He got up quickly and opened the chest. And as he opened it, he could see a little baby waving his arms through the opening of the silk cover and pushing it aside. Gwydion cradled the baby in his arms and made for the town, where he knew there was a woman who could bring him up. And he bargained with the woman to agree to take care of him.

She looked after the baby for that year. And at the end of the year he was as big as a two-year-old. By the end of the second year he was a tall lad, and could make his way to the court on his own. And, after he had come to the court, Gwydion took an interest in him. And the boy came to know him and to love him more than anyone. Then the boy was brought up in the court until he was four years old. And it would have been remarkable for an eight-year-old boy to be as big as he.

One day, the boy followed Gwydion as he was out walking. Gwydion made for Caer Arianrhod, his sister's fortress, and the boy followed him. After they had reached the court, Arianrhod stood up to welcome Gwydion and greet him.

'May God prosper you,' said Gwydion.

'Who is this boy at your heels?' she asked.

'This boy? He is your son,' said he.

'Oh! You! Why do you try to shame me, and keep on shaming me as long as this?'

'If the reason for your shame is that I have raised such a fine boy as this, there's no great reason for your shame!'

'What is your boy's name?' she asked.

'Indeed,' he said, 'he has no name yet.'

'Is that so!' she said. 'I tell you that he'll have no name – unless I myself give him a name.'

'As God's my witness, you're a wicked woman,' said he. 'The boy will have a name, whether you like it or not. You,' he said, 'are a woman who is bitter because she's not called a maiden, and from now on no one will ever call you a maiden.' And with that, Gwydion walked away angrily and went to Caer Dathl, and he remained there that night.

The next morning he got up, and took the boy with him, and went walking on the sea-shore between Caer Dathl and Aber Menai. And in the place where he saw seaweed and sea-girdle, he created a boat by magic. And from seaweed and dulse, he conjured leather, and he coloured it so that no one had ever seen more beautiful leather. Then he hoisted a sail on the boat, and he and the boy came to the entrance of the gate of Caer Arianrhod.

And then they began to cut out the shapes of shoes and to stitch them. Then the two of them were seen from the fort. When Gwydion knew they had been spotted, he changed their appearance completely so that no one could recognise them.

'Who are those men in the ship?' asked Arianrhod.

'Shoemakers,' they answered.

'Go and see what sort of leather they have, and what kind of work they do,' she said.

Then the messengers came to Gwydion and the boy. And after coming, they saw that Gwydion was colouring the leather with gold.

The Naming of Lleu

The messengers went back and told Arianrhod about this.

'Indeed!' she said. 'Take the measure of my foot, and tell the shoemaker to make shoes for me.'

And Gwydion made the shoes, not according to the measure, but larger. The shoes were brought to her. They were too big!

'These are too big,' she said. 'The shoemaker will be paid for these, but let him make smaller ones.'

Gwydion made another pair, but he made them smaller than her feet and sent them to her.

'Tell him that these shoes don't fit,' she said.

The messengers told Gwydion.

'Well,' he said, 'I won't make another pair for her until I see her feet.'

The messengers took this message to Arianrhod.

'Yes,' she said, 'I shall go to him.'

And she came to the boat. When she arrived, Gwydion was cutting out shapes from leather and the boy was stitching.

'Well, my lady,' said Gwydion, 'good day to you.'

'May God prosper you,' she said. 'I'm surprised you could not cut shoes to a proper measure.'

'I could not before,' he said, 'but I can now.'

At this moment, a wren alighted on the boat. And the boy aimed at it and hit it on the leg between tendon and bone. And she laughed.

'Indeed,' she said, 'that Lleu, that fair-haired boy, has a skilful hand to hit it.'

'Yes,' said Gwydion, 'God's curse on you. The boy has got a name now, and a good enough name at that: he is Lleu Llaw Gyffes, "the fair-haired one with the skilful hand".'

Then all the magic disappeared and the boat changed back to seaweed and sea-girdle.

'Truly,' said Arianrhod, 'you'll be no better off for treating me badly.'

'I have not treated you badly so far,' said Gwydion.

Then he changed the boy back to his own shape. And he himself took on his own shape.

'Is this how things are?' said Arianrhod. 'I say this boy will never bear arms unless I myself arm him.'

'As God's my witness,' said Gwydion, 'your own evil is the cause of all this trouble. But he shall bear arms!'

Then Gwydion and Lleu came towards Dinas Dinlleu. And Lleu was brought up there until he could ride every horse, and was perfect in feature and appearance, growth and size.

Then Gwydion saw that Lleu was pining for want of horses and arms, and he called the boy to him.

'Look, lad,' he said, 'we'll go – you and I – on an errand tomorrow. Be more cheerful than you are!'

'I will,' said the boy.

And early the following day they got up and went along the sea-shore towards Bryn Arien. And in the upper part of Cefn Cludno they travelled on horseback and came towards Caer Arianrhod. Then they changed their appearance, and made towards the gate of the fort looking just like two young men – except that Gwydion looked somewhat older than the lad.

'Porter!' said Gwydion. 'Go in and say there are poets from Glamorgan here.' Away went the porter.

'God's welcome to them! Let them in!' said Arianrhod.

There was great joy at their coming. And the hall was prepared, and they went to eat. After eating Gwydion and Arianrhod talked about stories and tales. And Gwydion was a good story-teller.

And when it was time for the entertainment to end, a room was prepared for them, and off they went to sleep.

Very early in the morning, Gwydion got up. Then he began to summon up his power of magic and enchantment. At first light there was a lot of coming and going, and the sound of horns, and shouting throughout the land. When day broke, they heard knocking on the door of the chamber and Arianrhod ordering that it should be opened. The young lad got up and opened it. In came Arianrhod, and a maidservant with her.

'Ah! men,' she said, 'we're in great danger.'

'Indeed!' said Gwydion. 'We can hear horns and shouting. But what do you suppose it is?'

'By my faith,' she said, 'we cannot see the colour of the sea because of all the ships that are crowded together. And they're heading towards land as fast as they can. What shall we do?' she asked.

'My lady,' said Gwydion, 'there's nothing to be done but shut ourselves inside the fort and defend it as best we can.'

'Yes,' said she. 'May God repay you! And prepare to defend yourselves – you'll find plenty of arms here.'

At that, Arianrhod fetched arms. And she came back with two maidservants carrying arms for two men.

'My lady,' said Gwydion, 'you arm the lad. And these maids will help me to arm myself. I can hear the sound of men coming.'

'I'll do that gladly,' said Arianrhod.

And she armed Lleu completely, and did it gladly.

'Have you armed the lad?' asked Gwydion.

'Yes,' said Arianrhod.

'I've armed myself too,' he said. 'And now, we'll remove these arms: we don't need them.'

'Oh!' she said. 'Why? The fleet is here and surrounding the fort!'

'Woman,' he said, 'there is no fleet.'

'Oh!' she said. 'Then what was this great gathering?'

'A gathering,' he said, 'to break your vow about your son, and to seek arms for him. And he now has arms – no thanks to you.'

'As God's my witness,' she said, 'you're an evil man. And many young men could have lost their lives in the turmoil you caused in this region today. I swear an oath that he'll never have a wife – not from all the women that are on this earth now.'

'Yes,' he said, 'you've always been an evil woman, and no one should help you. But he has had a name and arms, and he shall have a wife, too.'

Gwydion and Lleu came to Math and complained bitterly about Arianrhod, and Gwydion told him how they had obtained arms for Lleu.

'Yes,' said Math, 'we'll try – you and I – to create by our magic and enchantment a wife for him, out of flowers.'

By now, Lleu was full-grown and was the handsomest youth that anyone had ever seen.

And then they took the flowers of the oak, and the flowers of the broom, and the flowers of the meadowsweet, and from them they created the fairest and most beautiful maiden that anyone had ever seen. And she was baptised – in the way they baptised people at that time – and she was given the name Blodeuwedd, 'Face of Flowers'.

And during the feast to celebrate their marriage, Gwydion said, 'It's not easy for a man without land to support and sustain himself.'

'True,' said Math. 'I shall give him the very best region for a young man to have.'

'My lord,' said Gwydion, 'what region is that?'

'The region of Dinoding,' he said.

And that region is now called Eifynydd and Ardudwy. And the place in that region where Lleu made a court for himself was the place called Mur Castell, in the uplands of Ardudwy. He made his home and ruled there. And everyone was content with him and his rule.

And then, one day, Lleu went to visit Math at Caer Dathl. The day he set out for Caer Dathl, Blodeuwedd was loitering about the court, and she heard the sound of a horn. And after the sound of the horn, a tired stag ran past with hounds and huntsmen in pursuit. And after the hounds and huntsmen came a crowd of men on foot.

'Send a servant,' she said, 'to find out who this crowd is.'

Away went the servant and asked who they were.

'This is Gronw Bebr, lord of Penllyn,' they told the servant.

And the servant told all this to Blodeuwedd.

Face of Flowers

Gronw followed the stag. And by the River Cynfael he caught it and killed it. And he stayed to flay the stag and bait his hounds until dark. And as darkness fell, he came past the gate of the court.

'Truly,' said Blodeuwedd, 'we will be mocked by this lord if we let him pass to another region at this hour, without inviting him here.'

'True enough, my lady,' said the people of the court. 'The best thing to do is to invite him here.'

Then messengers went to meet Gronw to invite him to the court. He accepted the invitation gladly and came to the court. And Blodeuwedd came to him, to welcome him and greet him.

'My lady, may God repay you for your welcome,' he said.

They changed their clothes and went to sit down. And Blodeuwedd looked at him; and from the moment she looked, she was filled with love for him. He also looked at her, and he felt the same love for her as she had felt for him. He could not conceal his love for her, and he told her. She was full of joy at this. And that night they talked of nothing but the love and affection each felt for the other. And they did not delay but slept together that night. They passed that night together.

The following day Gronw asked leave to depart.

'Indeed,' she said, 'you will not go from me tonight.'

And they spent that night together too. And that night they discussed how they could remain together.

'There is only one way,' he said: 'pretend you are concerned for Lleu, and try to find out how he can be killed.'

The following day, Gronw again asked for leave to depart.

'Indeed, I don't want you to go from me today,' she said.

'Well, if you don't want me to go,' he said, 'I won't go. But I say there's a danger that the lord of this court will return.'

'Yes,' she said. 'Tomorrow, I'll let you go.'

The following day, he asked leave to depart, and she did not prevent him.

'Now,' said Gronw, 'remember what I told you, and speak earnestly to him, pretending you're concerned about him. Find out from him the way he can be killed.'

Lleu came home that night. And Blodeuwedd and he spent the day together talking and singing and enjoying themselves. And that night they went to bed together. He spoke to her once, twice. There was not a word in reply.

'What has happened to you?' he asked. 'Are you ill?'

'I am thinking,' she said, 'about something that you would not think about me: I'm troubled about your death. What if you were to die before me!'

'Well,' he said, 'may God repay you for your concern. But if God does not take my life, it's no easy matter to dispose of me.'

'For God's sake and my own,' she said, 'will you tell me in what way you may be killed? I'll remember better than you what you have to avoid.'

'I'll tell you gladly,' he said. 'It is not easy to kill me with any blow. And the spear that strikes me will have to be a year in the making, and no work must be done on it except during Mass on Sunday.'

'Is that certain?' she asked.

'Absolutely certain,' he said. 'I cannot be killed within a house, nor outside a house. I cannot be killed on horseback, nor on foot.'

'Indeed!' she said. 'And how can you be killed?'

'I'll tell you,' he said. 'A trough must be made for me on the bank of a river, with an arched framework about it, and it must be roofed well and warmly. And a billy-goat must be brought and placed near the trough. Then I have to place one foot on the back of the goat and the other on the side of the trough. Whoever strikes me in that position will kill me.'

'Indeed!' she said. 'I thank God for that. That can easily be avoided.'

As soon as Blodeuwedd heard this, she sent a message to Gronw Bebr. And Gronw worked on the spear, and a year to that day, it was ready. And that day he let Blodeuwedd know the spear was ready.

'My lord,' said Blodeuwedd to Lleu. 'I've been thinking about the way your death might happen. If I arrange to have a trough made ready, will you show me the way you ought to stand on the side of the trough and on the goat?'

'I will,' he said.

Blodeuwedd sent a message to Gronw and arranged for him to be in the shadow of the hill called Bryn Cyfergyr, on the bank of the River Cynfael. And she arranged for all the goats in the region to be rounded up and brought to the far side of the river, facing Bryn Cyfergyr.

The following day, Blodeuwedd said, 'My lord, I've prepared the framework and the trough, and they are ready.'

'Good,' he said. 'We'll take a look at them, gladly.'

The following day they came to see the trough.

'Will you go into the trough, my lord?' she asked.

'Gladly,' he said.

Into the trough he went and he bathed there.

'My lord,' she said, 'here are those animals that you said were called billy-goats.'

'Yes,' he said, 'have one of them caught and brought here.'

This was done. Then Lleu got out of the trough and put on his trousers, and put one foot on the side of the trough and the other on the back of the goat.

And Gronw rose up on the hill called Bryn Cyfergyr. He got up on one knee. And he cast the poisoned spear at Lleu and struck him in his side so that the shaft of the spear snapped, leaving the point inside him. Lleu leapt up then, and turned into an eagle, and flew up into the sky, screeching. And he disappeared from sight.

As soon as he flew away, Blodeuwedd and Gronw went to the court. And they spent that night together. And the following day, Gronw arose and took control of Ardudwy. After taking control of it, he ruled it so that both Ardudwy and Penllyn were his.

Then this tale reached Math, son of Mathonwy. And he became sad and troubled, and Gwydion even more than he.

'My lord,' said Gwydion, 'I shall never rest until I hear news of my nephew.'

'Yes,' said Math. 'God give you strength.'

Then Gwydion set out and began his journey. He walked through Gwynedd and Powys from one end to the other. After passing through every place, he came to Arfon and to the house of a peasant in Maenor Bennardd. He went into the house and stayed there that night.

The man of the house and his family came in, and last of all the swineherd arrived.

And the man of the house said to the swineherd, 'You, boy, did your sow come in tonight?'

'Yes,' he said, 'she's just come in to the pigs now.'

'What does that sow do, then?' asked Gwydion.

'Every day, when the sty is opened, out she goes. There's no sign of her after that, and no one knows where she goes any more than if the earth had swallowed her up.'

'For my sake,' said Gwydion, 'will you wait to open the sty tomorrow until I'm there with you?'

'Gladly,' he answered.

And they slept that night.

When the swineherd saw the light of day, he woke Gwydion. And Gwydion got up, put on his clothes and came with the swineherd to the sty. As soon as he had opened it, the sow jumped out and briskly walked off. And Gwydion followed her. She went upstream and made for the valley that is now called the Valley of Lleu. There she slowed down, and fed.

And Gwydion came under the tree where the sow was and had a look at what she was eating. And he saw that she was eating rotten flesh and maggots. Then he looked up at the top of the tree. And when he looked he saw an eagle in the tree top. When the eagle shook itself, maggots and dead flesh fell from it; and the sow devoured these. And Gwydion thought that the eagle was Lleu, and sang a poem:

The Eagle in the Oak

'An oak grows between two lakes
Darkening the sky and the valley.
If I do not speak falsely,
The cause of this was your "flowers", Lleu.'

And the eagle let itself fall until it was in the middle of the tree. And Gwydion sang another poem:

'An oak grows on an upland plain,
Rain does not wet it; it rots in the heat.
He has sustained a score of hardships
In its high branches, Lleu Llaw Gyffes.'

And the eagle let itself fall until it was on the lowest branch of the tree. Then Gwydion sang this third poem to him:

'An oak grows upon a hill,
A fair lord's sanctuary.
If I do not speak falsely,
Lleu will fall into my lap.'

And the eagle came down into Gwydion's lap. Then Gwydion struck it with his magic wand so that Lleu was in his own shape. But no one had ever seen a more sorry sight than he; he was nothing but skin and bone.

Lleu Betrayed

Blodeuwedd Punished

Then Gwydion made for Caer Dathl. And there all the good physicians that were in Gwynedd were brought to Lleu. Before the end of the year he was fully recovered. 'My lord,' said Lleu to Math, 'it's high time I won redress from the man who caused me such pain.'

'Indeed it is,' said Math. 'Gronw cannot go on in this way, withholding your recompense.'

'Yes,' said he, 'the sooner I obtain my redress, the better.'

Then the soldiers of Gwynedd were mustered, and they made for Ardudwy. Gwydion went on ahead of them, and he went to Mur Castell. When Blodeuwedd heard they were coming, she took her maidservants with her and set off for the mountain. She crossed the River Cynfael and headed for the court on the mountain. And so afraid were they that they could only walk looking backwards. And as they proceeded in this manner, they all fell into the lake on the mountain and drowned – all except Blodeuwedd.

And then Gwydion overtook her too. And he told her, 'I shall not kill you. I'll do something worse to you: I'll let you go in the shape of a bird. And

The Spear through the Stone

because of the shame you caused to Lleu Llaw Gyffes, you'll fear all the other birds. There will be enmity between you and all the other birds. They will feel bound to attack you and molest you whenever they come across you. But you will not lose your name: you will forever be called Blodeuwedd, "the Owl".' And this is the reason why the birds are hostile to the owl.

Gronw made for Penllyn. And from there he sent messengers. He asked Lleu whether he would accept land, or territory, or gold, or silver, as recompense for his injury.

'No,' said Lleu, 'on my oath to God, I shall not accept any such thing. This is the least that I'll accept from him: that he shall go to the place where I stood when he cast the spear at me, and that I shall go to the place where he stood. And that he shall let me cast a spear at him. That is the least I shall accept from him.'

This was reported to Gronw Bebr.

'Yes,' he said, 'I must do this ... My loyal noblemen and houseguard, is there anyone amongst you who will take this blow in my place?'

'Certainly not,' they said.

And because they refused to take the blow in place of their lord, they are called – from that day to this – the Disloyal Retinue.

'So,' said Gronw, 'I'll take the blow myself.'

And then the two of them, Lleu and Gronw, came to the bank of the River Cynfael. Gronw stood in the place where Lleu stood when he was struck by the spear; and Lleu stood in the place where Gronw stood. And then Gronw said to Lleu, 'My lord,' he said, 'it was because of a woman's shabby trick that I did what I did. In God's name, I beg of you: let me put that slab I see on the river bank between me and the blow.'

'Indeed,' said Lleu, 'I shall not refuse you that.'

'Yes,' he said, 'may God repay you.'

And then Gronw took the stone slab and put it between himself and the blow. Then Lleu struck him with the spear, and it went through the stone and through Gronw so that it broke his back.

And it was in this manner that Gronw Bebr was killed and there, on the bank of the River Cynfael in Ardudwy, there is a stone with a hole through it. Because of that, it is still called the Stone of Gronw.

And Lleu took control of the land for a second time and ruled over it in peace. And, as the old story tells, he afterwards became lord of Gwynedd.

And that is how this branch of the Mabinogi ends.

GLOSSARY OF WELSH NAMES

Arianrhod	*Are-ián-rode*: sister of Gwydion and Gilfaethwy, mother of Lleu Llaw Gyffes and Dylan
Arawn	*Áre-a-oon (-a-* as in *a*n): King of the Other World
Bendigeidfran	*Ben-dee-guíde-vrahn*: King of Britain, 'the Island of the Mighty'; brother of Branwen and Manawydan, half-brother of Efnisien
Blodeuwedd	*Blod-eýe-weth (th* as in *th*is): she was created by magic as a wife for Lleu
Branwen	*Bráhn-when*: sister of Bendigeidfran and Manawydan, half-sister of Efnisien, wife of Matholwch and mother of Gwern
Caradog	*Kar-ádd-ock*: one of the seven men Bendigeidfran left in charge of his kingdom
Cigfa	*Keég-vah*: wife of Pryderi
Dôn	*Dawn*: mother of Gwydion, Gilfaethwy and Arianrhod
Dyfed	*Dóve-edd*: a kingdom in south-west Wales
Dylan	*Dúll-anne*: one of the sons of Arianrhod
Efnisien	*Ev-níss-yen*: brother of Nisien, half-brother of Bendigeidfran
Gilfaethwy	*Geel-vá-ith-ooee*: brother of Gwydion and Arianrhod, nephew of Math
Goewin	*Go-aýe-ween*: foot-holder to Math
Gronw Pebyr	*Grów-noo Páy-br*: lord of Penllyn, Blodeuwedd's lover
Gwawl	*Góo-owl*: rival of Pwyll for the hand of Rhiannon
Gwern	*Góo-airn*: son of Matholwch and Branwen
Gwri	*Góo-ree*: the name given to Pryderi by Teyrnon
Gwydion	*Gwée-dee-on*: brother of Gilfaethwy and Arianrhod, nephew of Math, protector of Lleu
Gwynedd	*Gwín-eth (th* as in *th*is): a kingdom in north-west Wales
Hafgan	*Háve-gan*: a king in the Other World
Llasar	*Llás-are (ll = tl* as one sound): he gave Bendigeidfran the Cauldron of Rebirth
Lleu Llaw Gyffes	*Llay Llaoo Gúff-ess (ll = tl* as one sound): 'Lleu of the Skilful Hand', son of Arianrhod, husband of Blodeuwedd

Llwyd	*Llóoeed* (*ll* = *tl* as one sound): friend and avenger of Gwawl
Llŷr	*Ll-eer* (*ll* = *tl* as one sound): father of Bendigeidfran, Branwen and Manawydan
Manawydan	*Mana-wéed-anne*: brother of Bendigeidfran and Branwen, second husband of Rhiannon
Math	*Math* (*th* as in *th*ank): King of Gwynedd, uncle of Gwydion, Gilfaethwy and Arianrhod
Matholwch	*Math-óh-looch* (*ch* as in lo*ch*): King of Ireland; husband of Branwen and father of Gwern
Nisien	*Níss-yen*: brother of Efnisien, half-brother of Bendigeidfran
Pryderi	*Pree-dáy-ree*: King of Dyfed; son of Pwyll and Rhiannon, husband of Cigfa
Pwyll	*Póo-eell* (*ll* = *tl* as one sound): King of Dyfed; husband of Rhiannon, father of Pryderi
Rhiannon	*Rhee-ańne-on*: wife of Pwyll and mother of Pryderi; after Pwyll's death, wife of Manawydan
Teyrnon	*Táy-urn-on*: lord of Gwent Is Coed, adoptive father of Pryderi